AN Accidental
DATE WITH A
BILLIONAIRE

AN *Accidental* DATE WITH A BILLIONAIRE

DIANE ALBERTS

Entangled Publishing, LLC
2614 South Timberline Road
Suite 105, PMB 159
Fort Collins, CO 80525
rights@entangledpublishing.com

Indulgence is an imprint of Entangled Publishing, LLC.

Edited by Liz Pelletier
Cover design by Bree Archer
Cover photography by g-stockstudio and Beboy_ltd/GettyImages

Manufactured in the United States of America

First Edition April 2019

This one goes out to Sue, Lynn, Megan, Judy, April, and Sara. We're in this together, and I'm so happy I got you guys in my cohort.

Chapter One

This was the last place Samantha Matthews wanted to be.

The dentist with some random person's fingers in her mouth. Standing in the pouring rain in a sheer white shirt with no bra on. Hiking in ten feet of snow with only a pair of high heels to protect her feet. Stuck in an elevator with her ex from college. Heck, *all* those things combined, shoved into *one* day...

Would still be preferable to *this*.

Caviar and champagne filled the tabletops around her. Expensive perfume peppered the air. Priceless pearls dangled around necks. Diamonds twinkled in the lights. Gucci and Prada draped over artfully exposed shoulders. Stuffy voices with fake, trilling laughs topped off what was pretty much her worst nightmare. Nine out of ten times, people like the ones around her were concerned about one thing and only one thing. *Money.*

She'd been one of them.

When she walked away from her life of wealth and luxury, she'd left this whole scene, too. Fundraisers. Lavish dinners.

Balls. They were all ridiculous excuses to put on your best diamonds and show off how much more money you had than everyone else in the room.

She'd always won that contest, even at a young age.

Those days are gone.

Tonight, she'd forgone the private appointments for a custom gown and worn a dress she bought on clearance at Macy's last year.

She'd never been happier.

"More champagne, miss?" A waiter brandished a golden tray filled with whiskey and champagne like some kind of prize. Today it was.

Money might not buy happiness, but champagne sure made the world seem a little happier, even if only for a little while. "Thank you."

The waiter bowed and moved on to the next guest. A woman in last year's Prada sneered at Sam's clothing, so she lifted her glass in salute and took a long swig. The bubbles played on her tongue, tickling her throat as she swallowed. After the older woman turned away, Sam scanned the room for any signs of her target.

He hadn't bothered to show up yet…at least, she didn't think he had.

Of course, she didn't actually *know* him.

Her best friend Izzy texted her three hours ago, begging for Sam to bail her out. Izzy was running off with her boyfriend and getting married, unbeknownst to the rest of her family, but she had previously promised to attend this charity auction fundraiser and bid on her brother, whose assistant had mistakenly RSVP'd yes to the event.

According to Izzy, her older brother Andrew was a bit of a recluse. He wasn't big on crowds or getting auctioned off to the highest bidder, so he had no intention of *actually* going out on a date with any of the women here to bid on him. But since his sister was off marrying a guy none of them liked…

Enter Sam.

It was now *her* job to find Andrew Michaelson, bid however much money she had to on him, and save him from a fate worse than death itself—being forced into a situation he didn't want.

She took another sip and squinted at the stage. A handsome man was currently on the auction block, seeming as if he wanted to be swallowed up whole by the earth, and she winced in sympathy. She wouldn't want to stand there while people bid on her worth, either. Her fingers twitched in her lap, eager to put the guy out of his misery, but she flattened them on her thigh.

He wasn't the man she was supposed to save today. She mentally checked the schedule she'd read earlier, remembering that Izzy's brother would appear onstage last, so there were still several guys left before he popped up.

Turning her attention to her phone, she skimmed an email.

We had four people drop out of tomorrow's build at West Fourth Street. We are asking for any and all volunteers to step forward and fill their spots so we can still reach our goals. If you're available, please let us know by replying to this email.

Sam bit on her tongue as she mentally juggled her commitments for the weekend. She was booked to help at the animal shelter on Saturday, but they certainly wouldn't mind if she pushed her volunteer date to Sunday.

I'm in. See you at nine.

She checked the stage again, but they still had two more bachelors to go before they got to her man at the end. Picking up her champagne, she took another sip and opened Candy Crush on her phone. Time to demolish her record.

Somewhere between candy explosions, two more men, and a finished glass of champagne, Sam lifted her head, and her heart stopped beating for a second. The last man strode out, and he walked onto the stage like he owned the place—which, if she didn't know any better, she just might believe. He was incredibly handsome, in that he-must-be-an-actor-because-he's-too-pretty-to-be-normal kind of way. His muscles were huge and hard. His brown hair was slicked to the side with a hard part, and his square jaw spoke of a stubbornness only someone with equal stubbornness such as herself would recognize.

He wore a black tuxedo with a deep blue bow tie, a cocky expression, and walked onstage with his phone in his hand, typing furiously and ignoring the crowd of ladies who watched him with bated breath.

Hello, Izzy's brother.

Even she had to admit that, despite being totally not her type and way too sure of himself, he was hot with a capital *H*. Of course, he probably used those looks and his money to get pretty much anything he wanted, whenever he wanted it. It was what men like him did.

That was why she avoided them.

But those arms…

Forcing herself to stop admiring the way his jacket hugged his broad shoulders, she grabbed her orange flag off the table and waved it enthusiastically, happy to finally be at the part where she could bid and leave. Two hours was more than enough, thank you very much.

"One thousand, to the lady in red."

Izzy's brother lifted his head, checked out Sam, and returned his attention to his phone, typing even more furiously now.

A blonde lifted her flag, smiling at the guy on the stage.

He didn't seem to notice.

"Fifteen hundred to the woman in gold."

He didn't even lift his head this time.

Just kept typing.

She was *this close* to not saving him and letting him suffer through a date he clearly didn't want to go on, but she'd promised Izzy she would buy her brother, and she didn't break promises.

Not even ones she really wanted to.

She lifted her flag again.

"Two thousand to the lady in red."

Slowly, the man lifted his head again, locking eyes with her. For that brief second of eye contact, goosebumps rose on her flesh, and a surge of electricity tickled the nape of her neck.

What the heck?

The other woman raised her flag.

Sam stood, completely done with all this crap. She just wanted to finish bidding and get far away from Andrew and the weird way he made her feel. "I bid three thousand dollars," she interrupted.

"Three thousand dollars to the lady in red!" the announcer called out, smiling at Sam gratefully. She was the hostess, and she clearly appreciated the high bid.

Andrew's gaze turned intense.

She inhaled, her stomach tightening into a fist.

The other lady frowned and put her flag down, shooting Sam a dirty look.

"Going once, going twice. Sold, to the lady in red!"

Sam downed the rest of her champagne, ignoring the trembling in her thighs at the idea of approaching this god-like man, and gathered her purse. After she let him know he owed these fine people a bunch of money for the pleasure of spending an evening alone with himself—Izzy said she'd already arranged for her brother to cover the bid—she'd hit the road.

She had a house to build tomorrow.

As she made her way across the room, the champagne hit her, and a fuzziness warmed her stomach. The kind that warned you if you had another, you'd regret it in the morning. "Whoops," she whispered. "Too late."

She started to climb the stairs to the stage, but a man stepped in her way, offering her his arm. "This way, Miss…?"

"Matthews. Sam Matthews."

He grinned at her, giving her a discreet once-over. "I'm John."

"Hey, John," she murmured, treating him to the same perusal.

He was cute, in a safe, down-to-earth way. He was the type of guy she'd bring home for a night and never see again. Not guys like Andrew, who thought they owned the world and everyone in it. Guys like Andrew were too uptight. Too cocky. Too sure of themselves.

Maybe she should get John's number.

He bowed to her. "I'll take you to the cashier. Your date will be waiting for you there."

Oh. Right. She already had a "date."

"Thank you," she said.

Hopefully Andrew didn't mind her impatience to get out of here. Though, to a guy like him, that was probably pocket change. He wouldn't even notice the missing cash. But still.

Maybe she should have waited it out and tried to get the best price.

She *did* love the thrill of a good deal.

John led her to a woman who had an iPad Pro, a swipe thing for credit cards, and a big smile. "Congratulations, Ms. Matthews!"

Sam watched John go, regretting not asking for his number.

The bubbles had done their job, and she could use a night of fun.

"Ms. Matthews?" the woman said.

Sam took a second to be impressed that the lady had discovered her name in the ten seconds it took her to walk over to the makeshift cashier station. "Uh…" She searched the room for Andrew. Where was he? "Thanks."

"We appreciate the donation you made and want to make sure you know that all the money from tonight will be going to help those children with cancer that we showed on the screen before the bidding, as well as their families. Not a dime will be taken by us, the country club, or the staff of *Helping Children*."

Sam nodded, peeking over her shoulder.

Was he behind her?

Nope.

"That'll be three thousand dollars. Will you be paying with cash or credit?"

"Um, yeah, no." Sam choked on a laugh. "Neither."

The woman frowned. "I don't understand."

"Don't worry, you'll get your money. It's just…I'm here as a favor, you know? I bid on him so he didn't have to go on a date, because he's my best friend's brother. I did it for him. Well, actually, I did it for her, because I don't know him, you know?"

She stared at Sam, her mouth parted. "I…"

"Can I speak to Andrew? That'll fix this."

She blinked. "Andrew?"

"Yes, the man I just bid on. Andrew Michaelson."

The lady stared at her. Did she drink a little too much of that champagne and somehow freeze time inside her head??

After what felt like a million years, the woman shook herself slightly and cleared her throat, staring at something behind Sam. "Ms. Matthews…I fear there's been a mistake…"

"No, there hasn't. Like I said, you're getting your money," Sam interrupted, her cheeks hot because *everyone* in the room was staring at her. Everyone except the man she needed. "Andrew knows what's going on. If you get him and let him know—"

"I'm sorry, but that's not possible." The woman wrung her hands in front of her. "You see, Andrew already left. With his date."

His *date*? Sam's heart thudded against her chest, and her legs weakened for an entirely different reason now. "He... left? I...don't...understand."

"He left with his date. There was a last-minute schedule change, and Andrew needed to go first, so he changed places with one of our other men." The woman hesitated. "Andrew went first, Ms. Matthews."

The nervous guy. That had been Andrew.

Craaaap.

Sam's heart fell to her stomach, rolled out of her, and hit the floor with a sickening thud. If Andrew had already left, then she hadn't bid on him at all, and the man she had just offered to pay three thousand dollars for was her responsibility...and she needed to fork up the cash.

"But if I didn't bid on Andrew, who did I bid on?" she asked slowly, a bit too loudly.

"Me," a deep voice said from the distance behind her.

The masculine voice sent shivers down her spine, and her whole body tingled with something she didn't fully understand or welcome.

Slowly turning, she locked eyes with the man she'd bid on approaching her now. She hadn't been able to see this from far away, but his eyes were green. Like bright moss green. He also had a charming dimple in his chin that somehow softened his hard jaw. His expensive tux was paired with an equally expensive cologne, and he was even hotter up close than he'd been from a distance, totally breaking the Mona Lisa rule.

She had a feeling it wasn't the only rule he liked to break.

Chapter Two

Taylor hated being here and despised being auctioned off.

Even if the woman who bid on him was unbelievably intriguing. She stared at him with a combination of sparkling eyes and disdain, and for some reason he couldn't look away from that contradiction. She wore her long brown hair in a loose bun, with a few curls escaping around her cheeks, and her blue eyes hadn't left his face since he'd spoken to her. He suspected she was ten seconds from crying, screaming, or both.

But *why*?

She'd clearly been determined to win the bid for him, which meant only one of two things. One, she was hoping a date would lead to an "in" to becoming the future Mrs. Taylor Jennings, with access to his massive wealth. Or two, she needed something from him, and this was her big shot to try and get it. Either way, he wasn't interested.

His phone buzzed, and he glanced down, frowning at the message. "Unacceptable," he muttered.

The current hot-ticket impending bankruptcy on

the market, Granger Pharmaceuticals, had declined his extremely generous offer. Didn't they realize that without his help, they would be holding onto a useless building with millions of dollars in worthless equipment inside? If they didn't consolidate fast, they'd get a fraction of the worth for all the shit in their building they refused to let go of. For the life of him, he would never understand why people refused to admit when they gambled everything on something and lost.

"Excuse me?" the woman said.

His eyes were on his phone, but he could clearly see her annoyed, tapping foot below it. The shoe wasn't like the fancy designer ones women usually wore to this sort of thing.

Interesting.

"Sorry, that wasn't for you." He finished typing an angry response to his accountant before focusing on the woman again. Her cheeks were pale. "Are you ready for our date, Miss...?"

"Matthews. Sam Matthews."

"Sam." He cocked his head. "I'm Taylor Jennings."

She swallowed, wringing her purse in her hands. It, unlike the rest of her outfit, was not cheaply bought. It was Gucci. He always bought his mother Gucci. "I don't want to go out on a date with you," she blurted. "I just...uh...I don't know how to say this."

How unfortunate. He wouldn't have minded wining and dining her. Something about her drew him in, and he'd wanted to learn more about the woman who had spent three thousand dollars to go on a date with him. But apparently his "date" wanted door number two instead: a chance to ask him for money for some project or business idea.

Hiding his displeasure, he slid his hand into his pants pocket, holding a business card out for her. "Three thousand will get you about twenty minutes of my time."

Her jaw dropped. "Twenty minutes? Seriously?"

How much more time did she need to pitch a business proposal? "I feel that is more than enough time, but..." He shrugged lazily. "I suppose we could up it to thirty, if you insist."

"A thirty-minute date with you, all for the low cost of three thousand dollars," she said drily. "Wow, how *generous* of you."

Date? But she'd just said she didn't want a date with him. Damn, this woman was confusing. He couldn't read her, and she was still frowning at him as if he were gum under her shoe.

"I'm sorry, I must've misunderstood your intentions. Would you like a date? I can take you to a nice restaurant." He gave her a once-over again. That was definitely an off-the-rack gown and discount shoes, despite her expensive purse. But, *damn*, she wore it well. "You would probably like that, right? A special treat out somewhere nice?"

She reared back, nostrils flaring. "*Excuse* me?"

Shit, he'd pissed her off again. He seemed good at that tonight. Annoyed at this whole situation and himself, he gestured with his business card again. "Look, I don't care if you want a date or a business meeting. Either way, call my assistant, and she'll set one up for us. Bring a tight portfolio because I'm only giving you thirty minutes, no matter how much you pout at me."

She took the card angrily. "I won't be shortened to thirty minutes. You owe me a full date for the kind of money I'm paying for you."

"That's fine. If you want a date, I'll give you a—" His phone buzzed again with a counteroffer. It was ridiculous. "Son of a bitch."

As he typed furiously, her foot tapped faster.

After he finished, he glanced up. She had her arms crossed and was watching him with death in her eyes. He flexed his jaw, meeting her stare dead-on. Damn, the woman gave a good stare-down. He was half tempted to hire her and send her to Granger Pharm. She'd set them straight in no time at all. "Now, where were we?"

"You were ignoring me for your phone," she said with a fake politeness that grated on his nerves.

Determined not to show it, he forced a smile. "Ah, yes. Date or business meeting. Which is it going to be? Let's get this over with soon, too. I have a busy schedule the next few weeks."

"I want a date. Why would I want to *pitch* to you? I don't even know who you are or what you do for a living, and to be completely honest? I don't really care."

A laugh escaped him. He couldn't help it. He was so used to people kissing his ass for his power, money, or both—but she was refreshingly abrupt and clearly didn't give a shit about what he could give her. It was...*amusing.* "Okay, then—"

She interrupted him. "Pick me up tomorrow at nine?"

"At night?" It was a little later than he'd usually go for, but whatever.

"No, in the morning." She scribbled something on the back of the card he'd given her and handed it back. "Here. That's where I live."

He glanced at the address and tried to remember the last time a woman had asked him to breakfast—that he hadn't already slept with. Even more interesting. "All right. I look forward to our date, Sam."

She rolled her eyes at him. Actually rolled them.

"I'm sure," she said drily.

He said nothing—almost because he was afraid to interrupt what she might say next. So he waited patiently instead, though he couldn't stop himself from raising one eyebrow in humor as she continued to stare him down. For her, he might just have all night to continue this battle of wills.

An almost evil smile stretched her mouth, and he had to catch himself from smiling back at her. There was very little he loved more than a good challenge, and this lady had stubborn intelligence in spades.

"Oh, and dress casually," she added.

And there she did it again, surprised him almost speechless. He frowned. "Casually?"

"Yeah, you know. Jeans. Flannel. Boots." She tipped her head, her blue eyes flashing with something he could only assume was amusement at his expense. "Do you own those?"

"I own everything, darling, including your apartment building," he said cockily.

"My...?" Her jaw dropped. "Seriously?"

He gave her a wink. "See you at nine. Make sure you're ready, I don't like to be kept waiting."

"Because your time is *so* valuable," she shot back at him.

"You said it, not me."

For the first time in years, Taylor's well-oiled world had a monkey wrench thrown into it. He had absolutely no idea what tomorrow would bring. And he was shocked how much he liked the prospect. And the woman.

Chapter Three

Taylor had insisted on going out ASAP on a date she didn't even *want* to go on, and neither would he...especially once he realized what they were going to be doing.

But, hey, she'd paid three thousand dollars for the "privilege" to go out with the pompous asshat, so at least she'd get her money's worth out of him this way. Smiling, she tugged her hooded sweatshirt closed, watching the parking lot for any signs of the likely overpriced car he'd be driving. She couldn't wait to see his face when he realized what their "date" was going to be.

That man...he was as frustrating as he was attractive. It was time to bring him down a few pegs. What better way to annoy a spoiled rich man who had probably never had to worry about bills than to make him build a house for the poor? After she'd gotten home last night, she read over the rules of her date, and as long as her idea of a fun time didn't put his life in danger or require him to do something sexual, she was good to go. Their date didn't end until he dropped her off at home, so he'd be forced to help her make the world a better place.

A shiny black Alfa Romeo pulled into the parking lot, and she swallowed hard. Had he been kidding last night when he told her he owned her apartment building?

He pulled up, stopping directly in front of her. She started for the car, but he hopped out, rushing around the front. He wore a flannel shirt and a pair of jeans that appeared as if they'd just had the tags ripped off this morning. They still had the creases in places where they'd been folded.

Had he gone out and *bought* what she told him to wear?

"Let me help you," he said immediately, taking the toolbox out of her hand. He frowned down at it. "May I ask what's in the toolbox?"

She forced a smile. "No, you may not."

"Right." He flexed his jaw. "Let me guess? It's the giant chip that's normally on your shoulder? Did it not match your outfit, so you had to put it in a box?"

"No, it's for your huge ego," she muttered under her breath.

"Excuse me?"

Ignoring the question, she asked, "Should I sit in the back or the front?"

Hastily, he set the toolbox down and opened the passenger-side door for her. "The front, of course. I'll set these in the backseat."

"Why not the trunk?" she asked as she slid into the car. The leather seats were the softest leather she'd *ever* touched. Softer than silk, even.

"There's no room because that's where I put my huge ego," he said, smiling as he slammed the door in her face.

Sam: *0*

Taylor: *1*

After sliding the toolbox onto the backseat, he went around the back of his car and joined her inside. As he shut his door, he let out a sigh. She echoed it. He smelled even better today. Like Yves Saint Laurent. God, she loved that cologne. Why did *he* have to wear it?

The flannel he wore hugged his biceps, leaving nothing to the imagination. Those arms would come in handy today, hammering nails into wood.

"You don't like me," he stated, breaking the silence.

It wasn't a question. "Did you go out and buy that outfit special for today?"

He glanced at his clothes. "My assistant did. Why? Is it not what you wanted? You said flannel, jeans, and boots—"

"I know," she said, touching her seat belt.

"I did what you wanted," he added, frowning. "I wore what you asked me to."

"It's good. You're good," she said, trying not to laugh. He acted so worried that he'd done something wrong, and it was hard not to laugh when he clearly took everything so seriously. She was totally not that kind of person. *At all.* "Why do you care so much, though?"

"I always try to give a woman what she wants," he stated.

She bit her lip, biting back the snort trying to escape. "Of course, you do."

This guy…he was too much. On any other woman, his polite words and charming smile might work, but on her?

Nope.

But she had a feeling Taylor was a guy who didn't relinquish control easily, or ever, and she wasn't down for some dude telling her what she could and couldn't do, thank you very much.

No matter how hot he is.

"Do you like it?" he asked into the silence.

Crap. How long had she been sitting there?

She pursed her lips. "Like what?"

"The outfit," he said, narrowing his eyes.

They were so green. So…so…

No. She wasn't going there.

She wasn't about to wax poetic about his eyes, or the fact that they were greener than the grass in Scotland on a spring day. *Crap.* Too late.

"It's, uh, nice."

He shot her a frown. "Well, uh, thanks."

Even though she tried to hold it back, a smile broke out across her face like a mad case of the chicken pox—and just as unwanted. She couldn't help it.

She loved a quick-witted opponent.

"Wait a second. Is that a *smile*?" he asked, his eyes comically wide.

She killed it ruthlessly. "I don't know what you're talking about."

"Don't worry, I won't tell anyone."

She faced the window.

No more smiling, Sam.

She couldn't give him the wrong idea.

"Can I ask you something?"

Sighing, she gestured for him to go ahead. They still hadn't moved from the parking spot, and time was wasting.

He ran a hand through his hair, and it popped back into place obediently. "Why do you hate me?"

"How could I hate you when I don't *know* you?"

Dropping his hand to the back of his neck, he said, "You tell me."

She fidgeted, uncomfortable with this topic. "I don't like you, but I don't dislike you, either."

"I disagree," he argued. "I think you've made it pretty clear that you wouldn't like me even if I saved ten orphans from drowning in the Chicago River in front of your eyes."

She clenched and unclenched her hands in her lap, trying to decide how to respond to that statement. He wasn't wrong.

She didn't really like him. She tended to avoid people with a lot of money, and there was that devastating handsomeness of his...

But she didn't *hate* him.

Forcing her tone to stay flat, she finally settled for: "I don't know. I have a soft spot for people saving drowning children from certain death."

"Oh, great, I'll keep my eyes open, then."

She snorted out a laugh.

He still wasn't satisfied. "Is there another reason you don't like me, besides my lack of heroics with drowning children so far?"

She faced him again, crossing her arms in front of her chest. "Is there a reason you *want* me to?"

He hesitated, lifting a shoulder. "You don't know me, which you admitted. It bothers me that you made a snap judgment."

That admission made him seem a little more...human. "And?"

"And...I don't like it." He finally backed out of the parking spot, his brow furrowed when she didn't continue her sentence. "I'm not sure why."

"If it helps, I don't like a lot of people," she admitted, though it wasn't true. She was just trying to make him feel better. "Turn left."

Pulling up to the exit, he flicked his blinker on. "Oh, I get it."

She frowned. "Get what?"

"It's your thing. Not liking people."

She shrugged. "I don't have a *thing*. I just stopped caring about what other people thought about me when I..."

His brow lifted. "When you what?"

"When I walked away," she admitted, though it wasn't any of his business.

"What did you walk away from?"

"Nothing. Everything."

He side-eyed her as a UPS truck flew by. "Let me guess. You used to be an actress, with millions in the bank, but now you choose to live a simpler life in Chicago, in a rent-controlled apartment, without the cash you acquired with your beauty and luck."

He was closer than he might think.

She'd grown up rich. But when her parents stole money from their company and its employees and were sent to jail, she'd been shunned—with good reason. She'd been seventeen, in her senior year, about to go to college, and had to give up her Ivy League college acceptance because she could no longer afford the cost of tuition.

She lost everything all at once.

No one would ever be allowed to hurt her like that again.

She wouldn't waste her time forming relationships that would fall apart.

"Am I right?" he asked, chuckling.

"Nope, not an actress," she muttered.

"Damn."

"Sorry to disappoint you." She cleared her throat. "What about you? Were you born with a silver spoon in your hand and a diamond in your pacifier?"

He snorted. "No. I could barely afford to have a clean diaper on my ass."

"Really?" she asked, blinking.

He glanced at her, those green eyes of his pinning her to the soft leather seat more effectively than his actual touch would.

How did he *do* that?

"Why do you sound so surprised?"

Gesturing at him, she pursed her lips. "Because you've got the whole guy-who-never-struggled-a-day-in-his-life thing down to a tee."

He laughed. "To succeed in my world, you've got to be cutthroat. Confident. Ruthless."

Her parents had certainly been all those things, and more. "I'm sure you're good at that last one."

"I have to be," he said, shrugging. "It's my job."

She said nothing, tapping her fingers on her thigh.

He pulled up to a red light.

"Keep going straight. What do you do, anyway?" she asked slowly.

She didn't care. She was just making conversation.

"I acquire and consolidate businesses."

No. He wasn't *that* Mr. Jennings.

He must have mistaken her silence for confusion, because he continued on. "What that means is that I find companies that would fail, ones that are about to go under, and I buy them. Then I either turn them into something profitable or close them down."

She crossed her arms. "I know what it means." Figures he'd think she didn't understand.

"Okay." He approached a stop sign. "Straight?"

"Right." She hesitated. "I mean, right, as in turn right."

He got into the proper lane. "Where are we going?"

"You'll see," she answered. Boy, was he going to be surprised when they arrived. "Are these people whose companies you take willing to sell, or do you rip them from their hands by force?"

She already knew the answer.

He opened his mouth, then closed it. "A little bit of both."

"So…some are forced into it."

He nodded. "Unfortunately. In those circumstances, shareholders find me and ask me to step in."

"For a hostile takeover."

He frowned. "I've helped a few, but they're not the norm."

"And the employees…?"

Clearing his throat, he said, "Some lose their positions, but—"

"So, basically, you take people's jobs and companies away?"

He squared his jaw. "There's more to it than that."

"Is there, though?" She had no patience for people like him.

He didn't answer, and she glanced out the window, ending the conversation. He might try to make it sound better, but at the end of the day, he took people's dreams and lives, crushed them in his palm, and walked away with the profits…

Just like her parents.

Chapter Four

Damn, she *really* didn't like him.

Some small part of him liked that about her, but the bigger part wondered what the hell had happened to her in her life that she hated him so damn much. Had her family lost their business to a company like his? Had it been *his* company? That would, at least, explain the anger.

"How about you? What do you do?" he asked, breaking the steely silence. There was something about her that drew him in, and he was genuinely curious about her.

"I work for a small organization that helps struggling companies save themselves, and we create plans to help them succeed before the sharks sense blood in the water." She shot him a smile that wasn't so sweet. "Sharks like you, I guess."

Out of all the jobs in the world, she *had* to be on the opposite side of the ring as him.

He cocked a brow. "I see."

She might think he was a complete dick, but his company was fair, honest, and generous. He didn't get off on ending dreams. He did what he had to do, and he tried to make it as painless as possible for everyone involved.

"You make a living off ending businesses," she added, as if that proved anything.

"And you make yours from trying to help people who can't be saved, and in the end they walk away from me with less cash in their pockets than they'd hoped." He gritted his teeth. "So, really, who's the bad guy here?"

"Go left," she uttered.

He got in the proper lane. "I really am sorry for whatever I did to make you dislike me so much."

"You…" She relaxed her hands in her lap. "You never did anything to me."

Relief hit him in the chest as he waited for the light to turn green. The idea of him personally causing her harm didn't sit well in the pit of his stomach. "I'm glad. Believe it or not, I try to do good in the world, not bad. I never take my lifestyle and the things I've earned for granted. I go out of my way to help charities and donate to good causes, to do good with what I've been given."

She swallowed hard, meeting his stare.

For the first time, she didn't sneer at him with disinterest or anger. She almost had a light of understanding in her eyes. *Almost.* "I try to do the same."

"I can't imagine you have much to make up for in this world," he said honestly.

She turned away. "Well, you'd be wrong again."

His grip on the wheel shifted. Who *was* Sam, and what had she done in the past that haunted her? He wanted—no, *needed*—to know. "Seems like a common theme today."

"Probably common for you," she teased.

Holy shit, was she screwing with him?

He laughed, trying to match her lighter tone. "Yeah, you're probably right."

"I usually am," she added playfully.

The light finally turned green, and he pulled into the intersection, chuckling.

"Go straight."

He eyed the area they were in.

It was dilapidated, with broken windows and boarded-up doors. People huddled on stoops, watching his car as it passed, and he tightened his grip on the wheel.

"You okay?" she asked, a smile playing at her lips.

He forced himself to relax. "Yeah, of course. Why?"

"Are you nervous?"

Shaking his head, he stared straight ahead. "There's a difference between being nervous and alert. I'm alert."

She snort-laughed. How the hell did she make that sound so adorable? "Okay." She smoothed her hair again. "Turn left at the next street."

Up ahead was a lot of activity. A house was framed out, and people hustled around the woodwork, dressed in similar clothing to his. A few of them had Habitat for Humanity shirts on, and her choice of attire and the toolbox in his back seat made a hell of a lot of sense. "Is this where we're going?"

"Yes." She cocked her head and studied him, her nose crinkling up adorably as she did so. "Is that a problem?"

He had the distinct impression she'd *really* like it to be one. Unfortunately for her, if that was what she wanted, she would be disappointed. "No, not at all."

Pulling into the closest spot, he eyed the progress, mentally deciding where to best lend a hand. Out of all the places he could have expected his "date" to take him, this was pretty much the last scenario in his head. Most women wanted lavish dinners and expensive plays.

But not this one.

"I'll show you what to do and how to hold a hammer," she said, patting his shoulder as if trying to comfort him. "Whatever you need, I'm here for you."

Laughing, he slid his key out of the ignition. "No need."

"There's no shame in admitting you need help," she said, pushing her hair behind her ear.

He fought back a grin. "I agree, but I can hold a hammer."

"But can you *use* it?"

He locked eyes with her. "Oh, I can use it, all right."

Her cheeks reddened, and she crossed her arms defensively. "I find that hard to believe."

"No, you don't."

Cheeks bright red now, she refused to turn toward him. She was so pretty, sitting there with her long brown hair pulled up in a no-frills ponytail. She didn't have an ounce of makeup on, as if she'd purposely dressed to not impress, and yet she had the opposite effect on him.

"Let's go. They're waiting for us," she muttered, opening her car door.

He rushed around to the side of the car, trying to beat her to the toolbox, but *damn*, the woman moved quickly. By the time he reached her, she was already closing the door and switching the toolbox to her right hand. "Let me carry that—"

"I've got it," she said, tipping her nose into the air.

Reaching for it anyway, his fingers brushed hers before she jerked back. "But—"

"I *said*, I've got it."

Holding his hands up in surrender, he backed off. "Okay."

She stiffened even more. "You ready?"

"Yeah, hold on." He walked to his trunk, popping it open. Without saying a word, he pulled out the toolbox he always kept in his trunk, just in case. Old habits died hard. After closing the trunk, he nodded at her. "Now I'm ready."

Her jaw dropped. "You keep a toolbox in your car?"

"Always." He forced a smile despite her constant contempt toward him. "When I was in college, I worked construction."

She opened and closed her mouth, but no sound came out.

"My mom was on her own. She did her best to raise me and get me to college. She always worried about my future, so I secretly went out, got a job in construction, and used the cash to pay for college. She thought I got a scholarship, but the truth was I paid it all so she could stop worrying about me." He locked eyes with her. "Like I said, I wasn't born with a silver spoon."

After what had to have been a million years, she cleared her throat and stepped closer to him. "I...I guess not."

Someone passed by, and he waved. "Hey, Taylor."

"Max, what's up?"

The other man came over and clapped him on the back. "I didn't know you still did these things. How long's it been since we've seen each other? Four years?"

"Yeah, I think so," Taylor said, shame rushing over him. Had it been that long since he helped out? What happened to the time? What had happened to *him*? "Back now, though."

"Glad of it." Max walked backward, pointing to the left. "We could use some of your help with the framing. No one over there knows what they're doing—not like you do."

Taylor grinned. "I'll be right there." When he turned back to Sam, she looked like she'd swallowed nails. "You okay?" he asked, trying not to smile.

She fisted her hands. "You've...helped out before?"

He nodded.

"Then why didn't you have clothes to wear? And why haven't I seen you?" she asked in a rush.

He rubbed his jaw. "I got rid of the jeans I used to wear here when I got tar all over them and told myself I'd buy more before coming back. I can't believe it's been four years already...*shit*."

"I..." She cleared her throat. "I see."

As people shuffled from one task to another around

them, he shifted the toolbox to his other hand. Surprisingly, he was eager to get to work. It had been too long since he built something with his hands. "Were you coming here back then?"

"I'd have been in my junior year of college, so..." She pursed her lips. That meant she was deep in thought, and he'd give anything to know what was going through her mind. "Yes."

Damn. She was five years younger than his thirty-one. "I'm surprised I didn't see you."

She shrugged. "Not like you would have noticed me."

"I assure you, I would have noticed you."

She didn't meet his eyes.

"Can we start over?" he asked slowly, studying her for any kind of reaction.

Her face remained carefully blank. "What do you mean?"

"We can pretend we're meeting here for the first time, and we can just...talk. No preconceived impressions. No awkward conversations about bidding. Just two people, at a construction site, trying to put some good into the world."

She hesitated, shifting her grip on her toolbox.

"Hi, I'm Taylor Jennings." He held his hand out, waiting. The ball was in her court.

She didn't move. Didn't take his hand.

Well, there went that idea.

"All right," he said, pulling back. "Let's get this over—"

Moving fast, she caught his hand in hers, shaking it with a firm grip. "Sam Matthews. Nice to meet you."

He shook hers back, grinning widely. He couldn't help it. This victory was even bigger than the one he'd had in the boardroom Friday when he'd managed to peacefully take over a company *and* reassign half the employees to another recently acquired asset of his. *Why* did it matter so much to him, though, that she accepted his peace offering?

"Great to meet you." He let her go, his fingers lingering as he winked. "Now let's go build some shit. Maybe after we can grab a bite to eat."

"I…uh…actually had another stop planned in this date," she admitted, her cheeks red. "We're scheduled to help at the soup kitchen downtown at four."

He choked on a laugh, dragging his hand through his hair. "Seriously?"

She nodded.

"All right," he said, dipping his voice. "I'm looking forward to spending all day with you, Sam."

"Even though it'll be at these places?" she asked, gesturing behind her.

"Icing on the cake," he admitted. "I get to help while spending time with a compassionate woman. What's not to like?"

She scrunched her nose up as she turned away, clearly as ready to work as he was.

"Sam?"

She glanced over her shoulder at him. "Yeah?"

"Thank you for bringing me here." He swallowed hard. "It's been too long, and this is a good reminder to fix that."

She bit her lip. "You're welcome."

"Hopefully I can return the favor and remind you how to do something, too."

She spun on her heel, fully facing him, raising her brows in question. "Like what?"

"I don't know," he admitted, holding his arms out. "You're a mystery I can't quite solve, but I intend to do my best to figure you out."

She let out a small laugh. "Yeah. Okay. Good luck with that."

"Thanks."

As she walked toward a group of women, he watched her hair swing with each step and couldn't help but think that around her, he'd need all the luck he could get.

Chapter Five

Sam legit couldn't take her eyes off him. She'd done more watching and admiring than actual building, and it was all Taylor's fault. Why did he have to go and not be a jerk? She liked him better when he seemed like the kind of guy who never thought twice about the world outside of his penthouse. But *noooo*.

He had to go and *care*.

His muscles flexed as he hammered a nail into the wood, and a trail of sweat rolled down the side of his forehead and into his hair. The jeans he'd bought for their date hugged his butt in all the right places, and he'd rolled his flannel sleeves up to expose muscular forearms with dark brown hair speckled across tanned skin. A backup nail was perched in his mouth as he pounded steel on steel, and in complete honesty, she had to admit there was nothing more attractive in this world than Taylor Jennings using his hammer. He hadn't lied—he knew how to use it.

Damn him.

She was happy he wasn't a prick, but it made it so much

more tempting to forget who he was, and what he represented, for just a night…

No. She couldn't do that.

Lisa, a buddy who always ended up at the same builds as her, waved a hand in front of her face, fanning her. Sam snapped to attention, blinking. "Huh?"

"I said," Lisa enunciated, "you need some cooling off. Here you go."

Sam's cheeks flushed, but not from heat—though it was an unseasonably warm fall day in Chicago. "I'm fine."

"Yeah, sure you are," she agreed, grinning, "and so is he."

Sam forced her expression to remain calm. "I have no idea what you're talking about."

"That fine-ass man over there you're drooling over," Lisa said, pointing at Taylor.

Sam grabbed her hand, yanking it down. "Don't *point* at him."

Lisa laughed. "Who is he, anyway?"

"He's…he's kind of my date."

Lisa broke the laugh off. "You brought a *date* to Habitat for Humanity?"

"It's a long story," Sam muttered.

"I've got nothing but time," Lisa said, picking up a nail. "Tell me all about it."

Sam did the same, sighing, because to be honest, she *wanted* to talk to someone about this. "I went to a charity auction last night—"

"Big shocker there, you helping charities."

Sam ignored that. "—and he was on the stage."

"Why am I never invited to these types of things?" Lisa muttered.

"I bid on him, won, and brought him here to make him eat some humility pie. Turns out, I'm the one who needs it. He's actually a nice guy, and he's hot, and he had a toolbox in his car, which is even hotter, and now I can't take my eyes off him." Sam pounded on a nail, taking out her frustrations on the poor thing. "And he's hot. Like, really, *really* hot."

"You already said that," Lisa pointed out. She pushed her glasses into place with her left index finger.

"He's hot enough that it bears mentioning twice."

"True." Lisa chuckled and placed her nail gun against the wood, pulling the trigger smoothly. "How's Izzy?"

"I'm not sure," Sam said, frowning. "I've been trying to call her, but she doesn't answer. I'm hoping it's because she's too busy being happy, but with Don…"

Lisa shuddered. "I hate that guy."

"We all do," Sam agreed. There was just something about him that felt…off. Like everything he said was a lie he carefully orchestrated in order to get ahead in the world, but Izzy didn't see it. She loved the guy and refused to listen to anyone else.

"She'd be better off with a guy like that one," Lisa said, watching Taylor again.

Sam shook her head. "He's too risky. Guys who are too handsome usually want to control you."

"I'm all right with that. I'll take him off your hands if you want," Lisa said, sighing as she watched him.

Something Sam didn't want to name churned in her belly.

"By all means," she mumbled. "Help yourself."

"No use trying," Lisa said. "He's been staring at you all day."

Sam glanced at him.

Sure enough, he was checking her out.

The second they locked eyes, she expected him to turn away, but he smiled at her. He could totally be *People*'s "Sexiest Man Alive."

And he was grinning at *her*.

Sam broke the eye contact with Taylor after giving him a

small smile back.

"When's the last time you brought a guy home?"

"Uh…" She thought about it. "Like, a year. Maybe?"

Wow. Had it been that long? What the hell happened? Sure, she didn't do relationships, but she usually took time to go on the occasional date.

Lisa shook her head. "Take him home with you. A girl needs to have her fun, Sam."

Sam snorted. "No. Not with him."

If she went out on a date with someone, it would be with…Stewart, who worked at the coffee shop she always went to and never stopped flirting with her. He was cute, in a guy-next-door kind of way.

Stewart was *safe*.

Sam had a strict rule about life—she didn't take chances or make bad decisions that would come back to bite her in the butt.

Taylor had mistake written all over him.

"Shh, he's coming," Lisa said, smacking Sam's arm.

Sam didn't point out that she hadn't been talking.

"Hey," Taylor said from behind her. "Sam, right?"

She faced him, biting back a groan. He'd lifted his flannel up and swiped his forehead with his shirt, baring a set of abs that looked way too perfect to be real.

"H-Hey," she managed to say, tearing her attention away from his abs. So, he was still starting over with her. They were playing that game. "Yep, that's me."

He offered her a sheepish grin. The golden glow of late afternoon played with his hair, highlighting the lighter places to an almost blond color. "I saw you from across the way and couldn't help but notice how beautiful you are when you smile."

Her stomach twisted. It would be easy—so frigging easy—for her to do what Lisa said. The wind blew her hair in front of her face, cutting off her vision, and she was grateful for that. Not seeing him made it easier for her to keep her head on straight. "Thanks. That's very kind of you to say."

"This might be too forward of me, but I was thinking of hitting a soup kitchen after this and serving some food." He stepped closer, brushing a piece of hair off her cheek. "Would you like to come with me?"

Playing along, she pressed a hand to her chest and gasped. "But, sir, I barely know you."

"We can fix that." He gave her a once-over that should have set her on fire…along with her imagination. "Come with me."

He was so frigging smooth. *Ugh*. Maybe she should just forget about why she didn't usually date guys like Taylor. What's the worst thing that could happen—?

No, Sam. *Bad*.

"All right, I'll go with you." She swallowed hard, putting her tools away in her toolbox and closing the lid. "I'll talk to you later, Lisa?" she called, since her friend had moved to give them privacy.

Lisa nodded, watching Taylor from under her lashes. "Think about what I said, okay?"

Her cheeks heated. "Yeah."

Taylor offered his arm, his toolbox in his other hand. Even though she didn't want to touch him and tempt herself, she couldn't think of a good enough reason not to, so she slid her hand into the crook of his elbow. Despite his hard work, he still somehow smelled good. With that silky voice of his, he was a treat for the senses.

Not that she was interested.

"I meant what I said earlier."

She ripped herself out of her unwanted thoughts. "About what?"

"Thank you for bringing me here. I feel bad it's been

so long." He sighed, his forehead wrinkled. "It's just hard sometimes. I work over fifty hours a week, and by the time I'm done—I forget how important it is to give back. Being a Big Brother to a kid isn't enough."

"You have a brother?"

He laughed a little. "No, I have a sister. But I sponsor a child through the Big Brother program. Bring him to sporting events and stuff. He loves the Bulls and idolizes Michael Jordan."

Well, crap. His attractiveness multiplied by a thousand... *again*.

"Still, I should do more." He smiled at her. "Thank you for reminding me. I plan on coming back next week to help some more."

She swallowed. "Me too."

"Maybe I'll see you here, then?"

She shrugged.

"It could be our thing."

She swallowed. Did he want a *thing* with her?

"What does Lisa want you to think about?" he asked as they walked, arm in arm, their steps matching perfectly.

"She said I should bring you home with me tonight," she blurted out before she could change her mind and lie. "I told her it wasn't gonna happen."

He slowed his steps. "What? Why?"

"Why would I want to bring you home?" she asked in a rush, tightening her grip on her toolbox. "Or why won't I?"

Frowning, he stopped walking and searched her face for...something. She wasn't sure what, but hopefully he found it. "The second one."

"Because this isn't a real date. It's an obligation."

He let go of his hold on her arm, caught her chin, and tipped her face up to his. His fingers burned on her bare skin. There was no other word for it. "This feels pretty damn real to me."

Her breath caught in her throat. "I think we both know it's not."

"Then let's make it real."

She shook her head, legs trembling. "Taylor—"

"I like you, Sam. A lot."

A short laugh escaped her. She couldn't help it. She was just too darn cynical for her own good. "You don't even know me."

"But I want to, and that's huge for me. *Really* huge." He stepped closer, and her breath shortened, as if she were sprinting. "Go out with me on a real date tonight. Dinner. Your choice of restaurant. It can be as fancy or cheap as you'd like. Puerto's. Curry's. Applebee's. McDonald's. I don't give a damn, as long as you say yes."

The world spun around her because he was asking her out on an actual date, and the way he studied her...it was like he saw all her secrets, all her shame, and didn't care. That was impossible, of course, but *still*. For the first time in years, she wanted to ignore all the reasons she should say no, stop playing it safe, and spend a night in a rich, attractive, charming, charismatic man's arms—screw the consequences. She bit her tongue. Saying yes, was horrible, stupid, foolish, selfish, idiotic—

"Yes. I'll go out with you."

Well, *crap*.

Chapter Six

You're striking out, dumbass.

Taylor had taken a lot of women out, and he always knew just what to do. Flash his money at them. Buy them whatever they wanted.

But with *this* woman, none of that impressed her.

He'd never been an indecisive man, but with Sam…

It was an unsettling confusion. He prided himself on never losing his way, acting impulsively, or losing control. At a young age, he'd learned to hide his emotions. Life as the kid of the poorest single mom in an impoverished town had put a target on his back, and before he'd learned to control his temper, he had let some bratty kid get the best of him.

He didn't give a damn what they said about him, but the second that little fucker turned his insults toward his mother? It had been game fucking on. Taylor had unleashed the fires of hell on his enemy and broken his nose. He'd been pretty proud of it, too, until his mother had sobbed in the principal's office and he'd realized that his actions had only made things harder.

At that moment, he swore to never lose control again or make her cry. He'd been nine at the time. He had yet to break that promise.

But Sam threw him off.

He wasn't sure *why*…but she did.

She rubbed her bare arms, stepping into the darkness outside the soup kitchen. They'd been serving food for three hours now and had finally cleared the room of all hungry occupants. The sun had set, and there was a chill to the air that hadn't been there when they arrived.

Shrugging out of his flannel, he took a deep breath before sliding it over her shoulders.

Her mouth parted in surprise.

"You shivered," he said.

A small smile teased at her lips. "I'm cold."

"Hopefully not anymore."

She hugged the flannel close, taking a deep breath. "I'm a little better."

"Hungry?" he asked awkwardly.

She cocked her head adorably. "Starving, actually."

"Me too," he breathed, staring at her mouth.

She cleared her throat, hugging herself, and took a step back. Was it just him, or did she tremble? "Wh-Where do you want to go?"

"Would you rather decide?"

Shaking her head, she bit her lip. "You pick."

Fuck. "Okay." He opened the car door for her, smiling nervously. "I know the perfect place." *Liar.* "Not too fancy, not too plain."

Sliding into the seat, she smiled back at him. "Can't wait."

Where the fuck was he going to take her that wasn't too fancy or plain? As he opened his door, he remembered a place he went after work one night with his coworkers. It had thrown off his whole food schedule, but it had been worth it.

Grinning for real this time, he settled behind the wheel with a newfound confidence. It was about damn time. "Do you like whiskey?"

She blinked. "Not really."

"Irish beer?"

She shrugged. "I'm a sucker for a good Irish cider."

"Then you'll love where I'm taking you."

After buckling up, she glanced at her outfit. "Mind if we stop by my place first? I'd like to freshen up."

He swallowed hard. He'd offered to bring her earlier, but she'd refused. "Of course. It's on the way to my place, actually."

"Perfect." She fidgeted with the seat belt. "I'm sorry."

He side-eyed her and pulled onto the road. Traffic was surprisingly light. "There's nothing to be sorry for. I don't mind stopping."

"No, not for that. I'm sorry for misjudging you." Her fingers ran over the belt faster. "I had it in my head that you were an asshole, and I treated you like one when we first met."

"In all fairness, I'm an asshole most of the time."

"But not now?"

"Not when I'm with you," he stated easily.

Rolling her eyes, she let out a small laugh. There was something about that combination that thrilled him and made him even more determined to win her over. No one ever rolled their eyes at him anymore—they were too worried about offending him. "Wow. That was cheesy."

"I've got more where that came from."

She glanced at him out of the corner of her eye. "I bet they work on all the ladies, don't they?"

"I don't know. I don't normally have to work this hard." He shot her a teasing wink. "I feel like I've run twenty miles today."

She snorted. "Let me guess? Normally you wave money at women who catch your eye, and they collapse at your feet."

"Pretty much." He hesitated. "Though, sometimes I catch them before they hit the ground, if I'm feeling magnanimous."

She face-palmed. "Oh. My. God."

"Nope, just me." He pulled into her parking lot, not wanting to drop this fun, lighthearted tone they had going on. "You know, I just thought of something. The date is officially over once I bring you home."

She stared at the apartment. "At the end of the night."

"It didn't say that, it just said it was over after I brought you home." He slid the car into park. "I'm guessing it was to make it perfectly clear that if anything happened inside someone's door, it wasn't because of the auction."

"You don't think they wanted to prostitute the men?" she asked.

"Probably not. I mean, if so, they would have charged a hell of a lot more for me."

Closing her eyes, she shook her head. "Jesus."

"Nope, still just me," he quipped.

She dropped her head back against the seat, shaking it slowly.

He leaned closer, staring at her with a hint of a frown. "But, you see, I don't do second dates."

She nibbled on her lip. "Me either."

"Really?" he asked, surprised.

"Yep, I'm a one-and-done kind of girl."

He whistled through his teeth. "Nice." She was beautiful, kind, and charitable, but she didn't date. *Why?*

"So what are we supposed to do?" She pretended to think, tapping her chin and squinting. "If I go in, the date is over, but we didn't eat yet."

"Maybe we shouldn't go in," he stage-whispered. "As long as you don't go home, we're still on our first date, right?"

She turned to him, her eyes shining with…mischief? Or was that excitement? He had no idea, but damn it, he wanted to find out. He wanted to find out everything he could about Sam…and then some. "Pull back out onto the road before it's too late."

For a second, guilt hit his gut. But he'd meant what he said. He didn't do second dates. "But your clothes—"

"Are fine," she said, grinning. "Right?"

"You look absolutely perfect to me," he said with 100 percent honesty.

She snorted. "Don't lay it on too thick, charmer. You got the yes, so drive."

There she went again, shooting down his usual attempts at charming her, and making him want her even more. "Yes, ma'am." He buckled up and added, "Safety first."

"Of course," she said, bowing at him.

He bowed back as best he could while sitting. "My lady."

"Drive," she commanded frostily, sticking her nose up.

He, the guy who'd been voted most likely to be a Grinch by his colleagues at last year's Christmas party, was pretending to be a chauffeur and trying his best to make her forget that he was the very thing she didn't want him to be.

"Tell me something no one knows about you," he said, pulling out onto Broad Street.

"No one?" she squeaked.

"Or at least, not most people."

She fidgeted with her seat belt again. "Uh…let's see. I once had money. A lot of it."

"Had?" he asked carefully.

"Yes, had." She stared down at her lap. "Now I don't."

He didn't press. "My mom, as you know, was the opposite. She worked two jobs to raise me and almost killed herself in the process. There were weeks where we lived off spaghetti and ramen noodles."

She winced. "I hate ramen."

"I love it. I still eat it sometimes."

Shaking her head, she smiled wistfully. "And your dad?"

"Dead."

"I'm sorry," she breathed.

He hesitated. "My mom says he was nice, but he was probably a bigger asshole than me—after all, I had to have gotten it from somewhere, right?"

"I don't think you're an asshole."

"Give it time," he said, trying to keep his tone light. "By the end of the date, you'll be back to your original assessment of me."

She struggled with her response.

"True. Like, what kind of a jerk stares at his phone while he is being auctioned off?"

Well, shit. "You got me."

"Of course, I'm the jerk who was too busy emailing Habitat for Humanity to realize the guy I was supposed to bid on had already come and gone, so I guess we're both guilty."

"Yeah, maybe." He hesitated. "I was closing a deal."

She let out a breath. "Make a lot of money off it?"

"A good amount," he answered honestly.

She tapped her finger on her thigh. "Where's your mom now?"

"Uh…" He blinked at the abrupt change of topic. Clearly, she didn't want to talk about his line of work. Made sense, considering her own. "I suspect she's in her house on Park Drive."

She whistled through her teeth, acknowledging the costs of homes in that area. "Did you grow up in Chicago?"

"No, I actually grew up in Georgia."

She swiveled toward him, eyes wide. "Wait, *what*?"

"It's true. I'm a Southern boy, through and through."

"No way," she exclaimed, smacking his arm. "I'm from Savannah."

"No shit," he said, grinning.

"Dead serious."

"Why'd you come up here?" he asked.

The smile melted away at his question, and he immediately wanted to take it back. His lady clearly had secrets, and she had no desire to talk about them. "To get away."

He wisely didn't ask her what she ran from, even though he *really* wanted to. If he pushed too hard for information, she would walk away.

"I came here for a job. Once I got a salary and a bank account, I found a place for my mom, flew down, hauled her up north."

She swallowed. "You bought her a house on Park Drive?"

"Seemed like the least I could do for a woman who gave up her whole life to take care of me," he said, shrugging. "Anyone who thinks otherwise is even more of an asshole than me."

She shook her head. "Wow."

"She likes it here, especially the winters. We never had much snow in Georgia."

"What part?" she asked, watching him as he pulled into the parking garage closest to Fado Irish Pub.

"Rochester."

She winced.

"Yeah, not exactly the best area."

That rock hit his stomach every time he remembered his childhood home. It had been a hard life, and they'd survived. He'd made sure his mom never had to worry about money again.

"Every area is nice in its own way," she said, but she was being kind.

"Not where we lived." He shook his head.

"Let me guess. Now, you live near your mom in a penthouse?"

He turned left, heading toward a parking garage. Some

asshole in a red Corvette cut him off, so he slammed his foot on the brake. "*Maaaybe.*"

Laughing, she shook her head. She did that a lot when it came to him. He liked it. "With a fireplace, and a loft, and really fancy woodwork?"

"Are you spying on me?"

"I don't need to," she argued, wagging a finger at him. "You're so predictable."

"I'm not—"

"Uh-uh." She wagged the finger even more. "Don't even try to deny it. You probably wake up, hit the gym, shower, go to work, skip lunch, eat dinner over your desk, leave after eight, go home, work a little more, and hit the sheets by eleven every night during the week."

Well, damn.

"And the weekends?" he asked drily.

"You find a pretty girl, take her out, woo her with your fancy car and money, bring her back, turn on your fireplace, and take her to bed."

Again. Not far off. He rolled down the window, took a parking ticket, and pulled forward. "And after I get her in bed?"

"Then..." She swallowed. "Then when you're finished with her, you tell her you should do some more work, and she leaves—while giving you her number, which you'll never use—and you sleep in your bed, alone. Always alone."

Well, hell. She was right.

Somewhere between trying to make a name for himself and trying to succeed, he'd become something worse than an asshole—a *predictable* asshole. Worse than that, he'd forgotten how to have fun. He did the same exact thing, every damn day, on a perfect schedule, and he never deviated from the pattern.

When did he become so goddamn *boring*?

Chapter Seven

Going home with Taylor Jennings was a horrible idea. The worst. And yet, here she was, a few hours later, following through on the impulsive urge to make the most of this date. He pulled into a parking spot, his car much more at home here among the other Jaguars, Alfa Romeos, and Bentleys than it had in her parking lot with the Hondas and Toyotas.

It had been his suggestion to continue their date at his place because the contract said nothing about it ending if they went back to *his* place. So here they were.

Now what?

After giving her his flannel shirt, he'd only been wearing a white undershirt. That chest was nice, and she had an urge, one she'd been wholeheartedly denying, to touch it.

You only live once.

Maybe it was good to stop overthinking everything every once in a while, and just…

Do.

He wasn't her type *at all*. But it wasn't like she was gonna marry the guy or anything. She just wanted to see him naked.

They had been very clear on their one-date-only policy, so after tonight, she'd never see him—naked or otherwise—again.

He opened his car door, sliding out gracefully, and hurried over to open hers like a gentleman. She could have easily beaten him to it again, but this time she let him have his way.

Opening her door, he shot her a playful yet oh-so-sexy grin. "Having second thoughts already?"

What had been nothing more than revenge on some rich jerk she'd met at an event had turned into a magical evening with an attractive man who, for all intents and purposes, seemed to actually *like* her. Even more surprising, she liked him.

She didn't want to let go of that magic yet.

"Sam?" he asked, studying her closely. "Would you like me to take you home?"

That would be the smart thing to do.

The sensible choice.

She undid her seat belt with steady hands. "No, I want that champagne in front of the fireplace. Please tell me there's a fur rug where you seduce women."

Just like that, his grin returned as he offered her his help. "You've got me all figured out, huh?"

"Oh, yeah." She slid her fingers against his palm, electric tingles teasing her skin. "Definitely," she added a bit breathlessly.

But who could blame her? *Look at him.*

Dark hair. Bright eyes. Hard jaw. And a voice so deep it sent shivers down her spine. More important than all that, he'd made her laugh all night long.

No expectations. No attachments. No disappointment.

Just *fun*.

"Well, then, let's see if you're right."

Still holding her hand, he led her into the building. His grip was loose, allowing her to pull away easily if she chose to. As he walked toward an elevator, he pulled a swipe card out of his pocket with his free hand. The elevator doors opened, so he led her inside, swiped his card, and hit the thirty-fourth-floor button. She snorted to herself because a miracle was about to occur on the thirty-fourth floor. For the first time in a year…

Sam was going to get *laid*.

She should've shaved her legs.

"What's so funny?" he asked.

"Nothing, I just—" She broke off as the doors opened.

She'd expected a hallway, but the elevator doors opened right into his apartment.

Of course, he owns the whole frigging floor.

He tugged her inside his home, flicking the lights on. It was more of an understated opulence than an in-your-face kind.

Surprise. Surprise.

The floors were dark rustic wood in varying shades. The furniture was also dark, and the couches in front of a gas fireplace were leather—probably as soft as the leather seats in his car. The wall with the fireplace was covered in light brick, again in varying shades, and long lights on wires hung from the high, open ceiling above, illuminating the apartment with a soft, relaxing glow. Rubbing her arms, she approached the full-length windows that faced the Willis Tower. In the distance, the lights on the Lake Shore Drive Bridge flickered as cars sped over it.

Annnd here she was. In a penthouse for the first time in years. "Wow."

"It's what made me buy the place," Taylor said from behind her.

He stood just far away so that he wasn't crowding her,

and he'd been doing that all night. It was part of what made her so comfortable around him. She trusted him, which was ridiculous, really, considering they'd just met. There was an undeniable attraction that pulled her closer to him.

Did he sense it, too?

"It's beautiful," she said.

"I know," he murmured.

She turned and found him watching her. Her stomach knotted, and her breath hitched in her throat. It took everything she had not to glance down to see if she were on fire, as she burned so very hot for him. Nervously, she laughed and pressed her back against the cool glass of the window. It did nothing to save her from the flames he shot her way without even trying.

"So…" she started awkwardly.

He quirked a brow. "Yes?"

She was out of practice with one-night stands and had forgotten how to smoothly transition from the sexual tension to the actual sex part. Not to mention, she smelled kind of gross after working hard all day. Sliding her gaze to the side, her attention fell to the fireplace, and she latched on to it gratefully as a safe topic.

"I'm disappointed," she said, her voice cracking.

Out of the corner of her eye, his brow inched higher. "Why?"

She tipped her head to the left, pressing more firmly against the glass window. "No fur rug or clap-on lights."

He let out a soft laugh, running his hand through his hair. "They're not really my style."

"What is?"

He dropped his hands to her shoulders. "Understated lavishness."

Resting her hands on his chest, she nibbled on her lower lip, torn between wanting to be clean and fresh for him and the desire to move things forward toward her end goal—being naked and quivering with pleasure in his bed before hitting the road and forgetting all about him.

As if she would *ever* forget spending a night in Taylor's arms.

His hands gripped her waist…

He lowered his head toward hers…

His mouth moved until it was a mere breath away…

"I have a weird question," she blurted out seconds before his mouth collided with hers.

He froze, his fingers flexing. "Yes?"

"I…" She swallowed hard, knowing if she rose on tiptoe, their lips would be touching. "Can I…uh…shower?"

He cocked his head to the side. "You want to use my shower on our first date?"

"Yes." Hesitantly, she fisted his shirt. "And maybe…?"

He was hard. Hot. *Sexy.*

"Yes?" he murmured.

"Maybe you could shower, too?" Before she lost the nerve. "At the same time?"

His body tensed against hers. "Are you insinuating I smell?"

"I fail to see how you couldn't."

He half snorted, half laughed, and stepped back from her. "You have a point. As far as your request goes, yes, I have two showers, so that could be arranged."

"Great, that would be great," she said, cheeks hot because *that* hadn't been what she meant at all.

"Yeah…great."

They locked eyes.

Silence fell.

"Follow me," he said, pushing off the glass and fully removing his body from hers. "The guest bathroom is this way."

"Th-Thanks."

As soon as his heat left her, she wrapped her arms around herself, shivering. He led her into a bathroom that was larger than her apartment. As they passed a closet, he opened the door, removed a red towel, and held it out with a raised eyebrow. "Red okay?"

She took it, her fingers brushing his. Just that short skin contact sent a shiver through her entire body. "I love red."

"Me, too," he said, offering her a smile. He opened the shower door and gestured to the knob on the wall. The entire shower was encased in glass, and the tiles on the wall and floor were a deep gray color. "Left is hot, right is cold, the middle is lukewarm. Take as long as you'd like. I'll go wash up in the master bedroom. There's a robe hanging on the door, feel free to use it, and we could wash your clothing."

She swallowed. "How many women have worn that robe?"

"One."

She hesitated, hugging the towel to her chest. "Someone special?"

"You could say that." He shoved a hand through his hair. "I'll leave you to it."

He left, shutting the door behind him quietly. She stared at that closed door for far too long before undressing and getting in the shower. After she finished, she wrapped herself in the robe he'd mentioned, walked back out into the living room, and searched for Taylor.

He was nowhere to be found.

Still showering, she supposed.

Walking up to the window again, she took a second to admire the view. If only she were brave enough to go into the other bathroom, drop her robe, and climb into the shower with him. But what if he didn't want her to? What if he wasn't interested in her?

He almost kissed you earlier, her inner voice said. *But you just* had *to shower, didn't you?*

"I smelled," she whispered.

"What?" he asked from behind her.

She jumped, holding a hand to her racing heart, and backed up against the window. "You *scared* me. I thought you were showering."

"Sorry, I was already finished and was in the kitchen getting this," he said, his lips quirking up as he held out a glass filled with bubbling champagne. "Care for a drink?"

She took the offering and lifted it to her mouth.

He did the same.

"You're good," she said, licking the excess off her lips.

He cocked a brow. "What do you mean?"

"You've got this whole thing down," she said, gesturing between them. He, too, wore a robe, and…presumably…like her, was naked underneath. "The seduction thing."

His lips quirked into a half smile as he closed the distance between them, stopping when their toes touched. "You think?"

"Oh yeah." She nodded.

"If you think I'm that smooth, what comes next?"

"Well, if I were to guess, I'd say after you offer a girl a drink or two, you'd usually get her on that couch and slowly inch toward her, making sure not to move too fast because a guy like you always makes sure to take your time and ensure your advances are welcome…"

"Am I right in guessing there's a *but* in there somewhere…?" he asked, his gaze dipping to her mouth.

"Yes." She smiled and downed her drink, setting it on the nearby table. "*But*…might I suggest a deviation from habit?"

He finished his beverage and discarded the glass, stepping back slightly, giving her more breathing room—something she didn't want.

"Of course. I was already thinking we should take it sl—" He broke off when she caught his robe, halting his retreat.

"I don't want slow. I don't want caution."

I'm throwing away sensible and going for it.

He flexed his jaw, his eyes narrowed. He studied her like the lions on the Discovery Channel did a wildebeest. He had her in his sights, and any second now, he might pounce. "What do you want?"

"You." She curled her fists on his robe, not letting go. "I'd like to skip all of your normal steps and just get to the part where you make me scream your name out loud, against this window, and I'd like to do it now, please."

He stared at her, his jaw ticking, his breathing unsteady. But he didn't *move.*

Had she read him wrong?

"That is, of course, unless you don't want that." She laughed, letting him go. "Oh God, you don't, and I totally just threw myself at you, and you were just being nice and fulfilling your obligations, and I totally crossed the line just now, and I'm so frigging sorry. I'll just go now and die dramatically—"

His mouth closed over hers, effectively shutting her up and sending her into the stars because he tasted like the forbidden and champagne.

Yes, please.

Chapter Eight

This was a dangerous game he played.

He wanted tonight to be different than the others. Sam was special, one of a kind, and she deserved more than the usual seduction games he usually played. Somewhere between dinner and his place, he'd decided that he wanted to break his rules and spend more than one night with her. This needed to be a take-it-slow, long-conversations-by-the-fire, get-to-know-you type of encounter, and the best way to ensure that happened was to keep his damn hands to himself…

Yet here he was. Kissing her.

In his defense, she had all but demanded it, and what was he supposed to do? Let her keep panicking and watch her run off? Never to see her again?

He wasn't taking that chance. Taylor was a planner, not a risk-taker. As such, he'd come up with the perfect solution to their little problem. Neither of them wanted a second date, so he had come up with a way to avoid having one of those, while still getting to spend time with her: this date simply wouldn't *end*.

She couldn't go home.

He hadn't yet figured out how to propose the idea without sounding as if he was trying to kidnap her...but he'd get there eventually. While she'd been in the restroom at the restaurant, he'd made a few discreet phone calls and worked out a defense for every reason he could think of that she might come up with to argue that she couldn't stay.

Clothing. Food. Transportation. It was all covered except one thing:

She might not *want* to stay.

The only way to avoid that inescapable argument was to give her a reason to stick around. She wanted a screaming orgasm against his window? Fine. He'd give her one, but he refused to get one for himself. Refused to put her in the category she wanted to go in. He'd put her in a new one, and it had strict rules. He could give, but he couldn't take.

Not tonight.

If she wanted him to fuck her, she'd have to wait until tomorrow.

She'd have to agree to *stay.*

He deepened the kiss, his tongue finding hers. A soft moan escaped her, and he silenced it with his mouth, his hands exploring every inch of her body. The softness of her waist, the hard lines of her ribs, the seductive swell of her breasts... Never had he been so turned on by a woman during a simple kiss. He inched closer to her breast, only cupping her fully when she pressed against him, breathing raggedly. He closed his palm over her, letting her fill his hand as he scraped his nail over her nipple, dragging it slowly.

A gasp escaped her, and she arched against him eagerly. That small sound, that desire in her movements, hardened his already engorged cock, demanding he press against her and relieve the pressure. Breaking the kiss off and gritting his teeth, he kissed a path down her neck, ignoring the demands of his body.

This had to be done right.

No taking. Only giving.

He traced a path down her back, over the curve of her hip, and gripped her ass, groaning at how tight she was. Everything about her was specifically designed to make him lose control—something he never did. Not in life. Not at work.

Not in bed.

Relishing her soft body, he slid a hand between them, pressing his fingers against her—but keeping the protective fabric of the robe between them. She appeared to be naked underneath it, while he had on boxers and a pair of pajama pants.

Moaning, she writhed against him as he bit down on her neck gently. His hand moved in wide circles, teasing her. Even if she walked away after this and he never saw her again, as long as she remembered the way he kissed her and made her come…that was enough for him. His strokes quickened as he gently twisted her nipple, nibbling the sweet skin on her neck.

Those sexy little sounds escaping her hinted that she was close, so he repositioned himself to get her where she needed to go faster. The urge to press against her, to relieve the need building inside him, was overwhelmingly strong…but this wasn't about him, so instead he slipped his leg between hers, supporting her as her body tensed and lost control, and melded his mouth to hers.

As she came apart in his arms, screaming his name, he silently vowed that *whatever* she wanted from him, *whenever* she wanted it, he would find a way to give it to her.

No questions asked.

She collapsed back against the glass, her breath coming fast, and he allowed his lips to linger for a sweet second before ending the kiss, his arms still supporting her and his knee still between her thighs. Pulling back, he took it all in.

Her swollen red lips, her pinked cheeks, her mussed hair.

She appeared to have been thoroughly fucked, and he barely had a taste. His grip on her shifted up to her lower rib cage.

He was playing the long game here, and he had to remember that.

Forcing a grin even though his lack of release hurt, he said, "Would you like to spend the night in my bed?"

She blinked at him, mouth parted. "Wh-What?"

"Would you like to sleep here?" he called over his shoulder as he all but ran toward the wet bar. If he stayed too close, too long, he might not be able to behave. "I don't want this date to end, but I know you don't believe in second dates, so I figure we should just keep the date going. You should stay here. With me."

He sensed her approach but didn't turn around as he poured himself a scotch.

"I took the liberty of ordering you some clothing in a variety of styles and sizes, so you won't have to go home. When we're done, and you go home, you can keep it all, if you'd like."

She stiffened. "Are you trying to...*buy* me?"

"What? No." He set his glass down, his heart pounding because, once again, he'd screwed up with her. It was a miracle that she hadn't run in the opposite direction by now. "I would never. I just wanted to extend our date, and this is the only solution I can see in order to get another day with you by my side."

All signs of anger fled, replaced with something that could only be called reluctance. "Taylor..."

"I will, of course, sleep in the guest room tonight. You can have my bed all to yourself—it's more comfortable than the guest bed."

She rested her hands on the bar. The physical barrier between them was very welcome. Anything that helped him keep his hands to himself was a friend of his. "Did I do something wrong?"

Snorting, he faced her, trying to play it off like he wasn't fucking *dying* right now. He slid a glass of scotch toward her in case she wanted it and lifted his. "Of course not."

"Then…?" She hesitated. "Why did you stop?"

He locked gazes with her while drinking his scotch. It burned going down. He welcomed the distracting pain. "I gave you what you asked for."

She hesitated, clearly confused, if her wrinkled brow was any indication. He ached to reach out and smooth it for her but didn't trust himself touching her just yet. "And if I had asked for sex, would you have given me that?"

"Yes. No. I don't know." He flexed his jaw. "I want you to be different from the rest of the women I bring home. You *are* different, so I stopped after making you come because I want you to stay with me until we're both satisfied and not slip me into the 'one and done' file you probably have somewhere."

"I don't do second dates," she said, biting her tongue. "I told you that."

"I haven't either," he said coolly. "I'm not asking for forever. I'm not that guy. I'm asking to extend our first and only date over the course of a few days, so we can enjoy each other's company until we decide that it's over."

After taking a long gulp, she set the glass down. "You basically want me to move in with you, sleep in your bed indefinitely, and only wear clothing you picked out for me."

He hesitated before nodding. When she said it like that…

She let out a nervous laugh, pushing her hair back with a trembling hand. "Sounds a bit possessive."

Shrugging, he sipped his drink, trying his damnedest to ignore the twinge of pain that nagged at his soul. He'd never tried so hard before. He finished his drink and came around the side of the bar. He approached her, his heart pounding hard and echoing in his ears. "You're not moving in, Sam. Just spending a couple of nights on a first date with me."

She bit down on her plump, pink lip. "I like you. I do. But—"

"Don't do that. Don't add a *but.*" He caught her hand, pressing it to his heart. It sped up under her touch. "I'm going to let you in on something. You're my first."

Her brow crinkled again. "There's no way I'm your first one-night stand."

"You're my first non-one-night stand." Slowly, he ran the backs of his knuckles across her cheekbone, savoring the sensation of her smooth skin. "I don't mean to scare you, and we just met, but spending time with you is fun. I'd like to continue, if you're having fun, too, that is. If not, it's okay. I'll take you home."

When she didn't say anything, he grazed his fingers along her jaw.

Her eyes went wide, her breathing unsteady. Desire warred with fear, something he had every intention of wiping away...

If given the chance.

His thumb ran down her jaw, and he stepped closer, backing her against the bar. He kept the sides open, leaving her an escape if she so chose, but she fisted his robe and held on tight, swaying toward him. He pressed his body to hers, allowing himself one magical moment of her fitting against him so perfectly. Her eyes widened when he pressed his erection against her belly, splaying his free hand across her lower back.

"I want you, Sam. And I intend to have you."

She let out a soft moan. "You could have me right now."

He shook his head stubbornly, caressing her racing pulse. "Not enough. I want more. Stay on our date with me. Stay in my bed, Sam."

"I can't," she whispered, her voice cracking on a half laugh, half moan.

"Then our time will have to be over," he breathed, lowering his mouth to her ear, and pressed a gentle kiss to the lobe. "Or...you could stay the night, and maybe tomorrow I can show you just how much you'll scream with me buried inside your body."

She let out a groan, pulling her chin out of his grasp but staying where she was. He let his hand fall to the bar, missing her skin already. "I don't even *know* you. This is *insane*."

"We can get to know each other better if you stay."

She crossed her arms.

"Just think of it as a really long first date." He pushed off the bar, giving her space. She sagged against it slightly, her cheeks rosy. "Tell me something about yourself."

She tossed her hair over her shoulder with a flick of her head. "Not this again."

He laughed.

"I'm not sharing my deep dark secrets with you, Taylor."

"Then share the not-so-dark ones." He poured himself another scotch. "Like...do you cut in line sometimes?"

Her eyes widened. "What? *No.*"

"Do you steal from your office and bring home the good pens?" He smirked. "I do. All the time. Of course, I own the company, so they're mine anyway, but still. I take them home with me by accident, and my secretary has to order more and complains about people taking them. I never tell her it's me. I let her wonder and suspect everyone else, because it's funny."

She choked on a laugh. "That's horrible."

"I know," he admitted, smiling wider as his heart picked up speed for no explicable reason. "Yet, I still do it."

Shaking her head, she smiled. That smile?

It lit up the fucking room.

"You're incorrigible," she said, but the smile softened the words.

"I know," he said, shrugging. "And stubborn."

Snorting, she nodded. "I see that."

"Tell me one of yours now," he urged, sitting on the chair that faced the fireplace and the bar on an angle. "Anything.

Small. Big. Whatever."

She stared, and he sensed her retreat before she even took a step. But she surprised him by saying, "I haven't had sex with a man in a year."

"How about a woman?" he immediately asked.

She narrowed her eyes on him. "What? No."

"Just checking. I mean, you did say 'man,' so…"

Crossing her arms, she bit her lip. "I like men. I've just been too busy with my stuff to date."

"Me, too," he said. "But we can be busy and naked together for a few days, on our *first and only date*."

She shook her head. "Screw it. Where's your bedroom?"

Relief and victory crashed through him, giving him a rush stronger than he'd ever experienced before—even stronger than the time he'd cliff-dived in Colorado. "Down the hall, to the left. There's an extra toothbrush under the sink of the bathroom you just showered in. Help yourself. Your clothes will be here in the morning."

"Whose robe and toothbrush am I using?"

"Technically, my sister's, but she's never actually *used* the toothbrush, just the robe once." He paused, frowning at it. "I'm going to have to buy her a new one. She can never wear that robe again or even see it."

She played with the ties on the robe. "Definitely."

"You can keep it once we're done," he added. "It suits you."

"I'm basically Julia Roberts in *Pretty Woman*," she said, more to herself than to him. "Am I seriously going to do this?"

"Yes." He smiled. "But don't worry, I'll make it worth your while tomorrow."

She frowned. "But not tonight."

"Not tonight."

Shaking her head, she headed for the bedroom. "You're weird, Taylor Jennings."

Grinning, he called out, "You have *no* idea, Sam Matthews."

Chapter Nine

On a scale of stupid to idiotic, staying overnight at Taylor's place topped it. Sam's dreams and goals didn't include moving into Taylor's apartment because he'd promised her some pretty amazing sex as a reward. And yet, here she was…

She'd texted her neighbor, who would feed her cat while she was away, and had let her know she'd gone on a spontaneous trip. She'd left out the part about the trip being to one Taylor Jennings's *delicious* body. Lifting her chin, she walked out of his bedroom, shoving aside everything that had kept her up last night. He was nowhere to be seen.

"Taylor?" she called out.

Nothing.

Oh my God, had he *left* her here?

"Good morning, or should I say, good afternoon?" an all-too-familiar deep voice said from behind her. Just his voice alone sent a shiver down her spine and made her body ache for more of the pleasure he could give her so frigging easily it almost pissed her off. *Almost*. Because a girl had to respect on-demand orgasms delivered in such a handsome package.

"Sorry, I was tired."

"Obviously," he said with amusement. "I see you found the clothes I ordered."

"The obscene amount of clothing you ordered in five different sizes?" Snorting, she faced him...and lost her breath right away.

How did he do that?

Steal her thoughts, and breath, and intelligence?

He wore a black suit, a maroon dress shirt, and a black tie. His green eyes were strikingly intense, and his hard jaw held a hint of a five o'clock shadow she longed to get her hands on. "Well, I wanted to give you options. To be sure you'd find something you're comfortable in."

"Still. You bought too much."

He waved a hand.

She played with a metal sculpture on the table. "Are you going to work or something?"

He frowned. "Huh?"

"Your clothes..." She gestured at his suit. "Are you going to work?"

"Oh, that." He smoothed his suit, offering her a sheepish smile. "No. I had a meeting this morning, but it's done. I left a note for you, in case you woke up. I got back five minutes ago."

"I see," she managed to say, admiring how nicely his suit fit him from behind.

"You hungry?"

"Starving," she admitted. Her stomach rumbled loudly as if in agreement.

"Uh..." He glanced at it. "Clearly."

Sam's cheeks heated. "Shut up."

"Tell that to your stomach."

She followed him into the kitchen. He smelled as good as she remembered—no, *better*. "See? You're annoying me, and

I'm already regretting staying. I should've gone home last—"

Without warning, he backed her up against the cabinets, cupping her hips and pressing his body to hers in all the right places...and yet somehow managing to not touch her where she needed him most. "Shhh. None of that, now. If you're good, I'll make you very happy you stayed."

She gripped his biceps—geez, they were huge, hot, and rock-hard—and the kitchen spun around them at dangerous speeds. "I'm never good."

"Neither am I," he said, smirking.

"I was hoping you'd say that." The desire in her tone made her voice almost unrecognizable.

He pushed off the counter, leaving her alone and trembling, just like last night. "Let's see if we can get some food in that angry belly of yours. What's your order?"

"Hmm," she said distractedly, staring at the window where he'd, well... She headed that way, wanting to put some distance between them.

He tugged on his tie, loosening it while studying her. He had a way of looking at a girl that made her uneasy, bare, and impossibly turned on—all at once. "I pulled out the local Chinese place's menu. Unless you'd prefer something else? I just have a habit of Chinese on Sundays."

She trailed her hand over the wooden hutch against the wall. It was so smooth against her fingertips, despite its rustic, harsh appearance. More than likely, it was repurposed wood. "What's Tuesdays?" she teased.

"Pizza," he answered immediately.

She blinked, touching the vase on the hutch. It was old and probably very valuable. "Do you seriously have it all planned out to the day?"

"It started more as a habit than a plan, but now it's pretty firmly etched into my life, so I guess, yeah." He crossed his arms. "You make it seem like that's a bad thing, having a plan."

"What if you want pizza on Monday?"

He cocked his brow. "Then it tastes even better when I finally get it on Tuesday."

She laughed.

"I told you, I'm a patient man." He uncrossed his arms and walked back into the kitchen. "I'm perfectly willing to wait for what I want, especially when I know I'm going to get it in a day."

She swallowed hard. He'd made them wait a day for sex, and the anticipation was killing her. "Good to know," she managed to say.

The apartment was pretty open, so she could still see him despite his retreat—and that's what she was calling it. Every time he was close to doing something, to making good on his promise to have her, he backed off. The man clearly had a plan, and just as obviously, she wasn't privy to the details. Had he put a time limit on his satisfactory completion of this first date of theirs? Two days? A week? "Steal any pens at the meeting?"

Chuckling, he came out with a bunch of menus. "Not this time. Here. Pick whatever you want."

Rifling through, she found the Chinese one at the bottom. "I'd hate to deviate from your patterns. I'm not that kind of girl."

"You can be, with me, if you'd like." He tucked her hair behind her ear tenderly, the movement intimate. "You can be whatever you want with me."

One hand stayed on her hair, the other fell to her waist possessively.

"I'm not going to fall for you."

He touched her neck, teasing her. "I won't, either."

She laughed. "I know."

"Why the laugh?" he asked, frowning.

"Because the idea of you falling for me is funny. If you knew me and my background, you'd see how impossible that was." If she were to *actually* get serious with him, there was no way someone in the Chicago society wouldn't do their research and find out her past.

There was nothing a jilted society girl loved more than taking down a newcomer—especially one with her background. And she had no doubt that it would come out.

Her whole sordid past, aired like dirty laundry for all to see.

"Your past and social identity have nothing to do with my not falling for you," he said stiffly. "I choose not to fall for anyone because I don't *want* to."

"No big dreams of love, marriage, and having the stereotypical two-point-five kids?"

"Marriage is bullshit," he said.

She choked on a laugh. "Go on."

"It's nothing more than an overly emotional business contract." He leaned forward. "Think about it. You meet a bunch of people every day, but then you meet one you like, for some reason or another, and you offer to buy them a drink, or dinner, and you do it again, and again, until you finally merge your name and your bank accounts and split all your bills and save money. It's all one big transaction, rolled into one."

Her jaw dropped. "That's a bleak description of marriage."

"Does it make it any less true?" he asked honestly.

Well, at least she didn't have to worry about him falling in love with her.

That was a relief.

"Speaking of business transactions, I have a few rules of my own for ours."

He cocked a brow, his caress freezing instantly. "Go on."

"No 'society' events on this date." She clenched her teeth.

"No exceptions."

His frown deepened. "All right. May I ask why?"

She hesitated. Stick to the truth, or evade the question? In her experience, the more she stuck to the truth, the less likely she would be to risk unwanted probing. "It's not worth the attention I would bring to the table, since I used to be a famous actress and all that."

He stared, a muscle in his jaw ticking as he considered her. "You can trust me with more than the bare minimum, but I promise not to push for more than you're willing to give, and I'm a man of my word."

She forced a smile. "Thanks."

"Any more clauses?" he asked tightly.

She thought about it for a second and shook her head. "Should I run this by my lawyer?" she joked, trying to lighten the moment.

He didn't seem to get that. "If you'd like, sure. I can have my secretary draft up a document—"

"Oh my God, no." She let out a laugh. "I was kidding. It just felt so…formal."

"Well, when you think of it, personal relationships are just like business ones. Boundaries are laid. Expectations voiced. Agreements hatched and drafted." He ran the backs of his knuckles over her cheek, and the breath she'd been taking hitched in her throat. "They're not so different."

"That's a weird way to look at life."

He lifted a shoulder. "So. We have a deal? We're on a date until we decide otherwise—which, of course, we are both free to do at any given time. We don't go out to society events together, we won't fall in love. Did I forget anything?"

She shook her head. "I think that covers it."

"Good."

She bit her lip. "Well, now that that's settled—"

"It's tomorrow."

A nervous laugh escaped her. "Yeah—"

The words died on her tongue, because he kissed her, effectively swallowing them whole. She gripped his suit jacket, holding on tightly as his mouth moved over hers. He backed her against the nearest wall, his lips commanding her full attention as he tugged her shirt out of her skirt effortlessly.

Before he lifted it up, he ended the kiss, breathing raggedly as he searched her gaze for something. What? She had no idea. She kind of hoped he didn't find it, though.

"I want to make you come again, and this time I'm going to fuck you properly. That okay with you?" he asked, his voice low and steady as if he wasn't even slightly turned on right now when she was about to *die*.

She nodded, tugging him down by the back of his neck.

"Thank God," he mumbled under his breath before he picked her up, hauled her into his arms, and carried her into his room, his mouth never leaving hers as he walked.

She silently echoed the sentiment.

Chapter Ten

Even though it had only been hours since he'd kissed her—since he'd *met* her, even—it seemed more like he'd been waiting for years. Her sweet mouth pressed to his was all he'd been able to think about as he'd spent a long, sleepless night alone on the uncomfortable mattress in the guest bedroom—he *really* needed to buy a new one—regretting his impulsive decision to wait until today to touch her.

Lowering her to the comforter, he stepped back, appreciating the moment. Her hair fell down her back, her lips slightly swollen and her cheeks tinged pink. By the time he was finished with her, she would be quivering with pleasure and deliciously naked...and she'd forget all about ever wanting to go home. She was still hesitant, even now. Because of this, he took his time unbuttoning his shirt.

Clothing would only get in the way after he climbed on that bed.

Her lips parted as her gaze followed his hands. He took his time unbuttoning his shirt, giving her time to process what was about to happen. His mother had raised him to be a gentleman, to never pressure anyone or to move too fast—something he used not only in the bedroom, but in his everyday life, as well, because he didn't want anyone coming to him later on with regrets.

Especially not his Sam.

Shrugging his shoulders, he let his shirt hit the floor with his jacket.

Time to lose his pants.

Reaching the bottom of her shirt, she lifted it up.

"Don't," he commanded, his voice low.

She froze. "Why not?"

"I want to do it."

He'd take his time, too. Sam was a present he wanted to relish unwrapping. He refused to rush or deny her even a second of the pleasure he could give her.

Her hands dropped. "O-Okay."

His heart pounded so hard and fast he couldn't hear anything but his crushing need to have her in his arms. He undid his button, letting his pants join the rest of his clothing as he stood there wearing nothing more than a pair of boxer briefs. Pink infused her cheeks as she pressed her thighs together. Without hesitation, he rolled his boxers down his thighs, removed them, and stood straight.

Completely naked.

She sucked in a breath, readjusting her position, her thighs falling open slightly. "W-Wow."

After walking to the dresser, he pulled out a condom. She opened her arms to him, welcoming him. That enthusiasm was the best thing he'd seen in…well…maybe ever.

Ignoring her open arms, he climbed onto the bed at the bottom, starting at her feet. Slowly, he lifted her ankle to his chest, locking eyes with her. She swallowed, shivering as his fingers brushed the skin above her ankle.

Dragging the edge of his nail over her skin, he relished

the way she tried to move closer to him. He held her foot in place, lowering it to his lap as he skimmed his fingers over her calf, behind her knee, and back to her bare foot before doing the same to her other leg.

By the time he finished exploring her calf, she breathed quickly, and her body language spoke of an impatience he had no intention of listening to. As he moved up her body, his fingers followed, touching everywhere they could as they slid under her pencil skirt. Every sigh, every little noise she made, begged him for more, but he held back. This would be memorable, dammit.

Lowering her skirt, he was immediately rewarded with more skin. She was so flawlessly smooth, so tantalizing and soft. He slipped between her thighs, his fingers tracing a path he had every intention of following with his mouth. Over her calf, around her knee, up her inner thigh. He traced her lines through her panties, gently touching her core, and she moaned, letting her knees fall open in an unspoken invitation.

When he slid his hands under her shirt to lift it out of his way, she let out a low groan of frustration. "*Taylor—*"

"Nothing you say or do will make me do this any faster," he said, his tone even and steady despite the need coursing through his veins. "I don't rush. I don't lose control. I take my time."

To lose control was a weakness.

She bit her lower lip. "But—"

"No buts." He caught her chin. "I never let myself forget what I'm doing in bed, and today I'm blowing your fucking mind. I'll take my time, go slow, and by the time I'm buried inside you, you'll thank me for not losing my cool. Trust me."

A soft whimper escaped her when he slid her shirt over her head.

Her hard nipples fought against the confines of her sheer bra. The desire to forget his game plan was strong, but he ignored it because he never veered off course. Instead, he skimmed his fingers over her rib cage, undoing the clasp of her bra with a flick of his wrist.

As he caressed her skin, he gently lowered the straps of her bra over her shoulders and arms. Her back arched as he dropped it on the floor with the rest of their clothing. She was so beautifully curvy, his Sam. Flawless in every way.

Time for him to get a taste of perfection.

He lowered his mouth to her shoulder, closing his eyes and savoring her taste as she moaned and wrapped her arms around him. A warmth filled his chest, one he'd never known before.

Sliding between her thighs, he pressed himself against the only barrier that stood between him and paradise—her black panties, which he'd carefully left in place. She spread her thighs, letting him in as he kissed a path down her collarbone and back up to her other shoulder, taking a second to skim his fingers over the curve of her breast.

She moaned, writhing beneath him. "*Taylor.*"

His name on her lips, all breathless and wanting, fucking *killed* him. His body shook for a second, and for the first time he almost lost hold of the control he took such pride in. Slowly, torturously, he nipped the skin above her rosy pink nipple and lowered his mouth over the hard bud, scraping his teeth against it as he sucked it into his mouth. She cried out, squeezing him with her legs, and he stiffened as she tried to close her thighs around him.

Firmly, he gripped her legs and kept them where they belonged. As he released her nipple, he slid to the other side, leaving love bites along the way as he placed his hand between her legs.

Her breath hitched in her throat as his fingers moved in hard, fast circles over her core, lowering his body over hers as he went. A kiss here. A nip there. A scrape of the teeth above her belly button. Every sound that escaped her urged him on because she kept getting louder with each one. "Taylor," she moaned, burying her fingers in his hair and tugging him south.

Obligingly, he slid lower, her soft skin against his more intoxicating than anything he'd ever encountered. He lowered them down her legs and licked the spot to ease any pain he might have caused. She bit her lip as he scraped his teeth over her, moaning in pleasure. Her reactions called to him in ways he didn't fully understand and didn't really want to. Every sigh, every silent bite of her lip or tongue, only made him *need* more.

Kneeling between her thighs, he took a second to enjoy her feminine hips, large breasts, swollen lips, rosy cheeks, and hard nipples. The rosy lips between her thighs were wet and waiting for him. Needing to touch, taste, *feel* every inch of her, he thrust his tongue inside her folds.

"*Taylor*," she cried, pumping her hips up desperately.

Her body strained toward his, and his cock throbbed with a demand he could no longer deny. The tingling skin, the pulled nerves, the aching need in the bottom of his stomach…

There was *nothing* else like it.

Her body tightened around him, and she cried out as she came. He slid his hands under her ass and pressed his face even closer to her, lashing his tongue against her sensitive core.

She let out a strangled scream as she came again, her whole body going limp in his arms. This time he let her drop down to the mattress, her body replete. He grabbed a condom and rolled it into place. It took a couple of tries, since his damn hand was trembling too much.

Pull yourself together, man.

Gritting his teeth, he positioned himself in between her legs, her smooth, endless skin touching his in all the right places. Claiming her mouth as his, he buried himself inside her in one hard, smooth thrust. She cried out into his mouth, closing her legs around his hips as her body tightened around his cock, convulsing, squeezing as she orgasmed again.

He moved inside her slowly, for once in his life not counting the measure of his strokes or the breaths she held. He lost himself in the touch of Sam, her body closing around his, and he just...just...

Groaning, he closed his eyes, her hands roaming as he moved inside her, something happening to him he didn't fully understand and didn't really care to. All that mattered was this, Sam, and him...together like they'd been meant to be. When she came again, her body trembling, he pressed his thumb against her and deepened his strokes, his mouth never leaving hers as he led her up that mountain one more time... then held her as she dropped.

Her walls squeezed his hard cock, and he called out her name as blinding pleasure hit him so hard he literally collapsed on top of her, unable to see or move or breathe or *think*. He lay there with her naked body under his, his hold on her tight as he tried to catch his breath. With Sam, every stroke, every kiss, no matter how well planned out it might be, had been...different. *Special*.

Whatever the hell that meant.

Needing some space to think, he pushed off her abruptly and walked away, not looking over his shoulder as he kicked the bathroom door shut with the heel of his bare foot. Alone, he stared at himself in the mirror, dragging his hands down his face until they fell at his sides. Why had she hit him so hard, so fast? He'd lost control out there.

It *couldn't* happen again.

Chapter Eleven

"You can read that menu a million times, but Thai food won't magically appear for you," Sam said, grinning because he was so clearly off put by the fact that they'd broken from his routine, even though *he'd* been the one to suggest they go out to eat in the first place and insisted *she* pick the place. It wasn't until they'd arrived that she found out Wednesday nights were his Thai nights.

He set the menu down with a dramatic sigh for the third time. It was endearing, how set in his routines he was. Almost as endearing as his commitment to making her scream his name every night she'd been in his place—which had been three nights now.

Best three nights *ever.*

It was outrageous that she was basically living at his place, but what was even more shocking was the fact that she didn't want to *leave* yet. And he didn't seem inclined to kick her out, either.

She suspected he hadn't expected it to take this long, and to be honest, neither had she. She still wanted him, and, if anything, that desire had only strengthened with time. It was all his fault for being so frigging good in bed.

When would it go away?

Even while he was blowing her mind, he had his routines, and he stuck to them. He had probably never fully given himself over to someone else in bed. He liked being in full control too much for that. Despite her assurance that she wasn't the type of girl who would mess with his routines in the short time she would be in his life, this was one she really wanted to try to challenge. Once...just once...

She'd like to be in charge of that work of art he called a body. If given the chance, she'd climb on top of him, tie his wrists with satin, and have her way with him however and *wherever* she'd like. But he'd never allow it.

It wasn't his style.

Which was ironic, because giving herself over to a man wasn't *her* style, yet here she was, submitting to his every whim, unable to get enough of him. She never should've let him in, because some small part inside her was terrified she'd never completely get him out.

"I told you, I'm fine breaking from my usual routine," he muttered, tugging on his tie impatiently. He scanned the restaurant for the waiter, his jaw tense. "Are you ready to order?"

She picked up her menu, her mind still firmly on him tied up naked in his bed, at her full disposal. "Almost. I'm thinking maybe pancakes and bacon."

"But that's breakfast," he said, staring at her as if she'd lost her mind.

"And this diner serves breakfast all day. It's why I picked it."

He continued to stare at her as if she had a worm crawling out of her nose. Something told her he'd find that easier to accept than her dinner order. "Because you wanted breakfast. For dinner," he said flatly.

She nodded, biting the inside of her cheek to keep from grinning.

He was too frigging funny. He tried so hard to appear to be laid-back and chill, but he couldn't fool her. Not anymore.

Shaking his head, he picked up his menu again.

"Still no Thai," she said, guilt starting to overshadow her amusement at his displacement. Maybe they should just go—

"I'll do an omelet with home fries."

She blinked. "Oh yeah?"

"Yep. And hot chocolate with a lot of whipped cream."

He settled back against the red plastic booth with contentment written all over his face, as if he'd accomplished something huge. His childlike satisfaction tugged at heartstrings he had no right touching, so she focused on anything but *him*. Everything about this diner screamed the 1950s, but it probably wasn't actually that old.

"What are you getting?" he asked, shifting his weight slightly as he tugged at his sleeves.

"I'm not sure now." She pursed her lips. "Your order sounds pretty delicious."

A cocky brow rose. He always did that, and it should have annoyed her, that brow, but it made her heart race and her legs tremble, and she wanted to kiss him. *Ugh.* "It will be."

Her phone buzzed, and Sam pulled it out.

It was a text from her best friend, Izzy. *Vegas was a disaster. Will explain when back. Decided to take some time to myself.*

Frowning, she quickly typed: *Wait, what? Are you okay? CALL ME.*

Not now, I need time. No marriage, I'm still single, and I decided to stay in Vegas a few days. I'm okay, promise.

Sam hesitated. She was glad Izzy didn't marry the prick but upset her friend had been hurt. *But are you sure you're okay?*

Izzy sent a pic of herself sitting at a table in front of a fake Eiffel Tower, holding a drink and with a hot guy at her side also smiling. *I'm great.*

"Damn," Sam muttered, grinning. *Call me tonight*, she typed quickly.

"Everything okay?" Taylor asked cautiously.

"Yeah, it's my best friend. She went to Vegas to get married, but instead picked up this dude," she said, showing him the photo.

He nodded. "The one whose brother you were supposed to save?"

"None other," she agreed.

"I'm glad you were wrong that night," he said quietly.

She smiled at him. "Me, too. *He* wasn't, though."

Taylor laughed.

The waiter came, and they ordered their meals.

When Taylor gave his drink order, Sam smiled and said, "Same. Extra heavy on the whipped cream, please."

Once they were alone, he nudged her with his foot under the booth. "Copycat."

She shrugged. "I'm all right with that."

He laid his paper napkin on his lap and set his silverware on the placemat carefully. Despite the size of his bank account, he seemed just as at home in a Mom and Pop diner as a five-star restaurant. No matter where they went and what they did, he managed to keep his cool.

"How was work today?" he asked politely, giving her his full attention now that his silverware was in order. "Busy?"

"Very." She folded her hands in her lap. "I met with someone who is on the verge of losing everything and came up with a feasible solution to save it all with my boss."

He frowned. "What did you—?"

"Nope." She shook her head. "I'm not telling secrets to

the enemy."

For a second, he looked offended. "I'm not the enemy."

She snorted.

He avoided her gaze, straightening his napkin in his lap.

They fell into an awkward silence.

She picked up her napkin and silverware, regretting her words already. Sure, she was a bit biased, considering her past and her profession, but he wasn't a bad guy. In all honesty, he might be one of the nicest men she knew...

When he wasn't making her laugh until she cried or being so ridiculous she worried she might cause permanent eye damage from rolling her eyes too much, he was making her scream out his name in bed or saying things that were so beautifully sweet that he literally stole her breath away. He had an annoyingly persistent habit of doing that.

If she wasn't careful, she might die.

Then again...there were worse ways to go.

"Can I ask you a question?" she asked, breaking the tension.

He lifted his head, pinning her down with one of his intense stares. "Only if I get the same right, of equal or lesser value."

There he went again, turning a simple conversation into a business deal. "Fair enough," she allowed.

He inclined his head. "Go on."

"When did you set your routines? Like...with the food and stuff?" She tapped her fingers on her right thigh. "Was your childhood so set in stone?"

He shook his head. "My mother worked two jobs, sometimes three, and a different person watched us every night until I was old enough to take care of myself. None of them could cook anything besides spaghetti, and we never had anything exciting to eat unless it was the discount meat at the store that was about to expire. Even that was a rare treat saved for special occasions like birthdays or holidays. The pickings were slim and boring, but it was all I had, even through college."

She swallowed, the contrast between their childhoods slapping her in the face. Up until her senior year in high school, she'd had a personal chef who made her whatever she wanted at any hour of the night, even if Sam woke her up at midnight because she was hungry—something she was ashamed to admit she had done on a frequent basis.

Back then, she'd been spoiled rotten, and it had shown.

"So after college, I had money in my account and endless possibilities at my fingertips. It was—too much for a kid who had never had much of anything in his life at all. Overwhelming, even."

Nodding, she leaned closer. "So you came up with a system…"

"And stuck with it." He shrugged. "It works for me."

"Yeah. I get that."

The waiter brought their hot chocolates, and she skimmed the diner as he set them down carefully. There was a family of four a few booths over, and the children stared at their hot chocolates with wistful eyes. Sam had seen it enough to recognize it on sight. She waved at the youngest girl, and the child quickly turned away, picking up her water.

They all had water.

Water was free, after all, and kept a night out at a diner reasonable.

"Excuse me," she said, catching the waiter's attention as he walked away.

He came back immediately. "Yes?"

"That table over there with the family?" she said, pulling her card out.

The waiter nodded.

"Bring them all ice cream sundaes of their choice, and

hot chocolates, if they'd like. Then charge those items and the rest of their bill to this card, please." She'd been paid and eating a few meals at Taylor's place—which he refused to allow her to pay for—so she might as well pay it forward. "Don't tell them I did it, though."

He took the card, smiling. "Of course."

As he left, she turned back to Taylor, almost forgetting he was there. He stared at her with a look in his eye that trapped her breath in her throat, choking her.

"What?" she asked, fisting her hands in her lap.

He turned away, shaking his head. "Nothing. It's just…"

"It's just, what?"

"You're so fucking beautiful, inside and out, and to be honest, sometimes I don't know what to do with that." He flexed his jaw. "Or with you. You're just too good."

She snorted, her cheeks heating. "No, I'm not."

"Yes," he said, his voice low. "You're fucking amazing, and somehow you manage to have no clue just how special you are."

Well, there he went again. Striking her speechless.

Damn him.

Chapter Twelve

Sam fidgeted with the mug of hot chocolate, avoiding his gaze. She clearly didn't know what to do when he complimented her or tried to tell her how incredible she was. She usually either laughed it off or changed the subject abruptly to anything besides herself. Funny, because she was his favorite topic.

It was also the least frequently discussed.

Any time he touched on a personal topic or tried to coax a childhood story out of her, she clammed up. That was usually his game, too. Leave them guessing, keep them at arm's length.

But around her…

He wanted *more*.

Christ, he'd even been so desperate for information about her that he'd hired someone to dig into her past so he could find out everything there was to know about her, including the secrets she so desperately guarded. Upon receiving the report, however, he hadn't read it because it felt wrong.

"I believe I owe you a question," she said, her tone a little tense because she didn't want to answer it. But she would, because she promised. His Sam was a woman of her word.

He'd learned that.

"Ah, yes." He rubbed his hands together playfully, drawing out this rare moment where he was actually guaranteed an answer to some closely guarded secret of hers.

The waiter brought her card back, and she stole a glance at the family. He did the same. The mother was wiping her eyes, and the father had a comforting hand on her back as his daughter sipped at her hot cocoa. Their son dug into his ice cream enthusiastically.

"They said thank you to whoever paid their bill. I told them the couple who did it already left, so they wouldn't know it was you, like you wanted. It's really nice of you, though."

She made a small sound in the back of her throat as she added a tip and signed the charge slip. "It's nothing. Thank you for your help."

Nodding, he left them alone again.

"It's not nothing. It was really—"

She waved a hand. "Ask your question."

He sighed. She had a serious problem with accepting compliments. "Fine. We talked about my childhood and what made me the way I am today, so I think it's only fair I get to do the same."

Stiffening, she gestured for him to go on.

"You said that you used to have money, but don't anymore. I also have the distinct impression you don't like being around money or having a lot of it. Why is that?"

She covered her face with her hands, letting out a groan.

"It's of equal value," he argued. "It clearly shaped you into who you are today, just like my childhood did. So it's a valid question."

"I know," she admitted, pale enough to have seen a ghost. "But it doesn't mean I want to answer it."

He quirked a brow. He'd earned a question fair and

square and wasn't going to back down just because she didn't like the one he picked.

"My parents let money ruin their lives. They became so greedy, so impossibly greedy, that they forgot everything that mattered, just to add another comma or two to their bank account. They did whatever it took to get where they wanted to get, not caring how it affected others, and in the end, they lost everything…including me."

She played with her placemat.

What the hell had her parents done that had cost them their *child*? Had they broken the law in their quest for commas? Were they in jail? He had so many questions that had more questions inside them. He bit them back, letting her speak at her own speed.

"The worst part was, we had a lot of money already. They just wanted more." She took a breath, meeting his eyes for the first time since speaking. The pain, fear, and anger had him reaching out to cover her hand with his. And he didn't let go. "In the wrong hands, money can be evil, and it can lead good people to do really bad things. I decided after losing it all that I never wanted to have it again. I don't want to be tempted to fall into the same trap they did. I pay my bills, I do what needs to be done, and whatever is left over goes to charity. I don't want any extra commas in my account, not like them."

He gripped his knee with his free hand, understanding so much more about her now. Her dislike of money and all it could bring to the table made sense, but, selfishly, he couldn't help but wonder… Where did that leave *him*? After all, he had a lot of it, and if she wanted nothing to do with his wealth… "What happens if something goes wrong and you only have one comma in your account? Broken pipes? Check engine light on in your car?"

"I don't have a car, and I rent, so I'd call my landlord," she said, her shoulders relaxing slightly. She'd probably worried he would press for more information, but he'd promised not to. She wasn't the only one who stuck to her word. "But if there's an emergency, I have my credit cards. When I use them, I pay them off as quickly as possible, sometimes with one check, and then I go back to donating my extra cash. I don't want it sitting there, tempting me to splurge on crap I don't need. I prefer to live a simpler life."

"That's—admirable." He shifted, picturing the commas in his bank account.

Granted, he worked hard for that cash and had earned every cent, and he liked having a cushion after years of having nothing. But how much was *too* much?

At what point did he become just as greedy as her parents had been?

"Do you still talk to them?" he asked slowly.

She pressed her lips together, shaking her head. "No."

So, she'd walked away from them.

Her parents.

Over money.

If that was true, how could he expect her to stay with him? Wait. What the fuck? He didn't want her to stay. Not forever. Just for a little while. *Right?* Shit. He was losing his mind.

"What if you fell in love with someone who had it?"

She cocked her head, blinking. "Who had what?"

"Money," he managed to say, way too exposed.

Swallowing, she shook her head, not meeting his gaze. "I wouldn't."

"But if you did?"

"You're not understanding." She fisted her hands. "I *couldn't* fall in love with someone who would put me in that position. It's not me. It's not who I want to be. I don't want to be like them. And falling in love with someone wealthy... what if that changed me back to who I was? What if it made me forget what's important in life—the sun, the fresh air, the way the dew hits the petals of a rose in spring—and I started caring about the latest fashions, designs, and trends? *What if I lost myself?*"

He tightened his grip on her. Her hand was fisted so tightly under his that she would probably have permanent nail marks etched in her palms. "What if you stayed the same? What if you made him a better person, too? Don't you think that's a possibility?"

"I don't know," she said honestly. "But I'm not sure I'm willing to find out for something I'm not even sure I believe in."

He frowned. "What do you mean?"

"You're talking about believing in the power of love and ignoring everything you know about yourself in the hopes that it would be enough to save you. I don't really buy into that whole thing, ya know? I don't really believe in love saving a soul from going bad."

Well, neither did *he*.

She pulled free of his touch, letting out a small laugh. "Enough serious talk?"

"Hell yes," he gratefully replied. "Let's talk about anything else. Birds. Dogs. Cats. The weather."

Laughing for real now, she pushed her hair behind her ear. She always did that when she was nervous—either that or biting her lower lip. "I know the perfect topic."

"Yeah?" He leaned in, smiling. "What is it?"

"You owe me two questions."

She was right. He'd asked follow-up questions to his one allotted one. "All right. Fair enough. Shoot."

"Did your mom ever remarry?"

Damn, she'd had that one loaded, aimed, and ready to fire. "No. My mom didn't even date. I think she never got over losing my dad. There were never any men around." He picked up his hot chocolate, curling his hands around the mug. "To this day she has no interest in finding someone to spend her life with, no matter how many times I tell her she should. I don't want her to be lonely."

She picked up her drink, too, inhaling the scent. "Why would she be lonely?"

"I don't know, I work a lot. Don't get over there as much as I'd like."

Nodding, she sipped her drink.

"That was one." He leaned back. "Next?"

"What jobs did your mom work?"

He teased, "I should have asked that one. I want to know what your parents do."

A hint of discomfort touched her expression before she chased it away with a flat, complacent smile. "Another question for another time, maybe."

"Fine." He sighed. "She did anything she could. Waitressing, receptionist, clerk, fast food." He moved his mug out of the way because the waiter approached with their food. Breakfast for dinner. Who the hell did shit like that? Oh, right. *Sam.*

"When I went to college, she got a job as a custodian there so I could get free tuition. I only had to pay for room and board—which is when I got that construction job I told you about and lied to her about getting a scholarship that covered those fees. She did everything she could for me and my sister to succeed, and now I do everything *I* can to make her comfortable without her having to lift a damn finger to take care of anyone else ever again."

Her beautiful eyes showed all her thoughts. She was so unbelievably expressive, while somehow managing to be one of the most closed-off people he'd ever known. "Some people might say that makes you a pretty amazing person, too."

"I say it makes me a person who repays his debts, and

nothing more."

She *cluck*ed her tongue. "Whatever."

The waiter gave them their plates. His footsteps echoed on the white and black checkered tiled floor. The walls were covered in the same patterned tile, which became disorienting after a while.

She cleared her throat. "I'm going to ask another question. How and when did your dad die?"

The family of four walked down the sidewalk in front of the window. The father held on to the little girl's hand, and the boy held on to his mother. They seemed so happy. So... normal. Would he ever have that? Shit, did he *want* to have that someday?

Not too long ago, he would have said no.

But now...he wasn't so sure.

"You don't have to answer that, never mind," Sam said, probably mistaking his silence for evasion rather than introspection.

Tearing his attention off the family, he finally answered her question. "He died when I was four. My sister was a newborn. A drunk driver hit him when he was walking home from work. He never even saw it coming, from what I've been told."

She touched his hand, her fingers lingering over his. "I'm sorry."

"Yeah, me too." He cleared his throat. "I don't remember him at all, but supposedly he was a great guy. I guess it's true. I mean, why else would my mother mourn him for the rest of her life, right?"

"Love," she said quietly.

He twisted his lips. "I guess."

"Do you believe in love?" she asked quietly.

"Yes and no." He cut into his omelet. "I believe that people love one another, and that they have feelings, but I don't believe in soul mates or any of that shit. I don't believe that my mother couldn't have found more love in her life if she wanted to. If you can fall in love once, and you lose that love, why not just go out and get another?"

She choked on a laugh. "I don't think the modern image of love is replaceable like that."

"If it isn't, why do so many people remarry or date new people?" He lifted a shoulder. "Seems pretty damn replaceable to me. Why else have a type?"

She blinked. "What do you mean?"

"Everyone likes a certain type of person and gravitates toward that, right?" he asked. "Blonde. Brunette. Slim. Curvy. Funny. Quiet. We all have a type we find attractive."

She nodded.

"So, if you lose the 'love of your life' to death or divorce or whatever, just go out, find a new blonde, or redhead, or artist—whatever gets your rocks off—and try again until you get it right. Eventually, one of them will stick around."

"You can't just go around buying people at the store and returning them until you find the right fit. People's *time* can be bought," she argued. "Not the person themselves."

He lifted a brow. "I politely disagree. Everyone can be bought, for a price."

She didn't answer.

Chapter Thirteen

The next night, Sam was still no closer to being tired of Taylor than she'd been when she went home with him the first night. They'd just finished eating and were curled up on the couch with each other in front of the fireplace, watching the flames dance against the brick backdrop.

Taylor's home was starting to feel like—well, home.

The floors were no longer overkill. The fire no longer seemed lavish. The soft leather wasn't exotically soft to her, but rather how leather was supposed to be. Little by little, she was getting accustomed to the lifestyle that Taylor lived, just like she feared.

Was she losing herself?

"Camping?" he asked, his voice tight. "You can't be serious."

She smiled, loving the sound of pure horror in his voice, and turned off the fear that plagued her. "Not just camping, but also rebuilding nature trails, since they've been destroyed by disrespectful people over the past few years. We're hoping to give underprivileged kids a place to enjoy nature, right here in the city. Isn't that amazing?"

He stared blankly at her.

"Don't worry, we'll have a tent."

Taylor crossed his arms. "Oh, yay. That makes me feel *so* much better."

She couldn't help it. This time, she full-on laughed at him. "Have you never been camping?"

"Why would I want to sleep outside with the bears, snakes, and bugs when we have the ability to build these magical things over our heads, which house us from those elements, called *buildings*?"

She snorted. "I don't think there are many bears in Chicago."

"No, just criminals who like dark parks and dilapidated trails because no one smart goes in them at night," he retorted.

She choked on a laugh that she unsuccessfully tried to hold back.

They'd been discussing plans for the weekend, since they were clearly still on their "first" date, and when he'd asked her what charitable event they were working at, he'd clearly not been expecting the answer she'd given him. Who would have thought the unstoppable Taylor Jennings was afraid to sleep outside?

"I'm not afraid," he said, frowning.

Funny, she hadn't meant to say that out loud.

"I just don't think it's a bright idea to sleep in a dark Chicago park in the middle of winter," he added crankily.

She lifted her brows. "It's November."

"And freezing outside."

She sipped her wine. "You don't have to come. I can go alone."

"But we're still on our date."

She stared at the white wine in her glass, swallowing hard. "Well, all good things must come to an end eventually, right?"

It was true. They had been avoiding the topic and all, but eventually this date of theirs would have to actually end. Maybe now was a good time. Even as the words crossed her mind, her heart objected. She wasn't falling for him or anything, but she wasn't *done* yet.

Was he?

He climbed on top of her, tugging her body beneath his on the couch and removing the wineglass from her hand. His hand slid under her butt, and he slipped his leg between hers, pressing against her in all the right places. "*No.*"

She curled her hands on his shoulders, her breath hitching in her throat. "No?"

"No. Our date continues on. Unless...?"

Her lids drifted shut, and her stomach tightened in anticipation as she gave herself over to his soft touches, forgetting all about ending dates and camping and anything at all besides him.

"...Unless you want to be done, Sam?"

She shook her head quickly. "N-No. Do you?"

"Fuck no." He kissed a path down her neck. "When do we leave for some fun camping?"

She closed her eyes again, arching her back as he moved even lower, over the curve of her breast. The relief swelling in her chest that he wasn't done with her yet was as undeniable as her fear that he would someday answer differently. She wanted that. She *did*.

Yet...she didn't.

"Five," she managed to answer.

"Okay." He lifted her shirt. "Can't wait to sleep outside with no protection."

Choking on a half laugh, half moan, she lifted her arms so he could pull her shirt over her head. He did, tossing it onto the floor. "You know, I'm going to have to go home and sleep in my bed eventually."

"Yeah." He scraped his teeth over her nipple. "After our date is over."

Shutting off her mind, she tried to let herself enjoy the moment—they'd both agreed that this was temporary, fun—but the longer they dragged on this "fun" date, the more they risked someone getting hurt.

• • •

Taylor extended his hands toward the fire, sighing as the heat took away the numbness just enough for them to hurt again. They'd both worked all day and immediately met up to come here and build some fucking trails, only stopping once the sun went down to strap head lamps to their foreheads so they could continue to make improvements. Sam, like usual, pushed through the cold and tiredness without flinching and had been the last one to call it quits.

He didn't count, since he had only continued working to stay by her side. She constantly amazed him with her willingness to give, her complete unselfishness, which ran her life and drove every choice she made. She was always the first to offer help and the last to walk away. She did more than anyone else in the world, and yet she still strove to do more.

To *be* more.

She was an inspiration and a lesson in humility, all in one beautiful package.

Around her, he came up inadequate, and he was inspired to match her kindness and her heart, something he suspected he might never do. No one would ever be as good, as giving, as Sam.

Maybe that was why he didn't want their "date" to end.

He lived by a strict set of rules, and they existed for a reason, despite how much Sam liked to tease him...and they shouldn't be broken, because they keep life in order and under control. People liked to say that life wasn't yours to control, that God had bigger plans than you could touch. He called bullshit on that.

You could control your life, if you wanted to. Set some boundaries, lay down some rules and routines, and you'd know what was coming next because you planned it that way.

But with Sam...

He was veering off the plan.

Here he was, in the woods, in the dark, vulnerable to attack, all because he didn't want to end his time with Sam. This wasn't something he could control.

What the hell was wrong with him lately?

"Feeling better?" she asked, nudging him with her shoulder playfully.

No. Forcing a smile, he shrugged. "Yeah, the heat is nice."

"So are the s'mores." She handed him one, which he took without hesitation.

He hadn't had a s'more since middle school, at a sleepover he'd gone to at Mark Greer's house. His mother had picked him up before the actual sleepover part because he hadn't wanted to sleep in someone else's bed. Even back then, he'd been set in his ways.

Yet he was in the woods.

Without a bed.

She broke the silence again. "Come on, admit it. You're having a *little* bit of fun."

As he took a bite of the warm treat, chocolate and marshmallow spewed out the sides. He popped the whole thing in his mouth, hoping to avoid more of a mess. Though sloppy as hell, they were fucking delicious. "The snacks aren't so bad," he said into the flames.

Neither was the company.

"You've got...here." Grinning, she reached out and

smoothed her finger over his chin, sticking her finger in her mouth and sucking on it. "There. All gone."

He wasn't sure whether to be turned on by her sucking on her finger or embarrassed he'd had marshmallow on his face in the first place. He settled for an awkward combination of the two that had him shifting his weight on the cold, hard ground. "Thanks."

She closed another s'more, popping it into her mouth effortlessly. She managed to do it without making a mess all over her face, unlike him. She wiped her hands on her jeans, picking up her canned beer and taking a swig. He hadn't had canned beer since college, when he'd been too poor to afford anything else. Apparently, when saving the world and planting some trees, volunteers liked to unwind afterward with cheap beer, fires, and s'mores.

Who knew?

"Are you doing Habitat for Humanity tomorrow afternoon?" someone to her left asked her.

"I…" The uncertainty was clear in her eyes. She wanted to say yes but worried he might not want to. He refused to be the one to stop her from living her life, so he grinned and nodded. She turned back to the woman who asked her the question, relief in her eyes. "Yep. We are."

"And, of course, the soup kitchen after," he added.

He remembered her mentioning that she did that every Saturday night. Every other weekend was also her time at the animal shelter. She cleaned the cages, petted the puppies, and snuggled the cats. She'd skipped last week for him, but he would make sure she didn't have to do so again.

The woman was nonstop.

Was she ever selfish? Did she ever do anything for herself, just because she wanted to? Maybe that was why he hadn't ended things yet, even though she was upending his life. Maybe he wanted to give her something that was good for her for once—like on-demand orgasms, for starters. Maybe he was her little act of selflessness. It was the least he could do.

"Great." She beamed at him. "Then dinner at Fado?"

"Sure, I'd like that."

Maybe Saturday nights would become Fado nights.

But would he *want* to go without her?

She turned to talk to the woman, but she didn't stop touching him, as if she needed the connection. Scarily enough, he did, too.

Run. Run fast.

"You two dating?" some dude asked from beside him, watching Sam with what could only be described as desire.

Taylor stiffened, something unfamiliar and hot poking him in the gut. "Yeah, something like that."

"Lucky," the guy said, taking a sip of his cheap beer. "Most of us have tried to get her to go out with us, but she's always too busy saving the world. To be honest, I was kind of hoping tonight was my night. Fires. Beer. Nature. The stars. But clearly, I'm too late."

The firelight played with her hair. It highlighted the contours of her face, softening the curve of her cheek. She was absolutely breathtaking, inside and out. It was no wonder this guy had a thing for her.

Taylor did, too.

He faced the guy, trying not to let jealousy get the best of him. After all, soon enough she'd be on her own again, and he'd be nothing more than a memory of that time she had a really long date with some rich asshole. Would this dude be her next one-night stand? Would she break the rules for him, like she had for Taylor? "Yeah, you are."

"Roy." The man shook his hand.

"Taylor," he said as politely as he could.

Roy nodded. "Nice to meet you. You new to all this?"

"Yeah, she kind of dragged me into the life," he said,

tipping his head toward Sam.

"The things we do for love," Roy said, watching her too closely for Taylor's liking.

Love? Hell no. Despite his continued desire to be in her company, that was one emotion he had no intention of ever visiting. "I don't lo…"

"Come on," Sam said, urging him to his feet.

He let her lift him, following her into the darkness, away from the crowds, despite his itching need to tell Roy he had it all wrong. The second they were out of earshot, he broke his silence. "Unless you're bringing me out here to fuck, I think we should go back. We shouldn't wander too far from the group alone."

"Stop being such a dad," she whispered, tugging him along.

He gritted his teeth at her insult, the feel of her skin on his warring with his annoyance with her, and, if he was being honest? With himself. "Did you seriously just call me a—?"

"Shh. Here. Look."

He glanced around impatiently. Nothing but trees and darkness. He'd much rather be back at the campsite, admiring the way the firelight played with her beauty—or better yet? In his bedroom, naked in bed with her in his arms. "At?" he asked testily.

She glanced at him sharply, surprise at his tone evident in her eyes. Gently, she tipped his chin up with her fingers. "Look at the sky, Taylor."

He lifted his head.

Stars twinkled above. "Wow."

"Isn't it beautiful?" she asked, her face turned up to the sky.

He swallowed hard, watching her profile. "Stunning."

She turned to him, catching him staring. The smile froze on her lips, and she didn't move. "Taylor…"

"Yeah?"

"Thank you for coming with me tonight, and for this whole week with you on this date. It's been...great. Really great."

He reached for her slowly, pushing the hair out of her face. "You say that like this is goodbye."

She pressed her hand into his cheek. "Maybe it should be, before things get bad. You know?"

Something a hell of a lot like denial settled in his throat, choking him, despite his mirroring worries he'd had earlier tonight. She kept talking about ending things, but he wasn't ready, damn it. *Not yet.* He tightened his grip on her. "Why?"

"Because things like this only go on for so long before they have to become something else, or end, and we know this can never be anything other than what it is."

"It doesn't have to be, though." He ran his knuckles down her smooth cheek, his heart beating yet somehow hurting so much it seemed impossible for it to do so. "Not tonight."

"Okay." She cleared her throat. "But I just wanted to tell you here, under the stars, that I will never forget you, Taylor Jennings. Not even after we've moved on with our lives."

Grief hit him hard in the chest at the same time as denial punched him in the stomach, making it twist into knots that threatened the s'more he'd just eaten. There was no way in hell he was ready to let go of her yet, but he'd have to soon. There was no other choice. Avoiding her gaze and the way her sad eyes made him want to promise things he couldn't, he pulled her into his arms and rested her cheek on his chest.

Being out here in nature, with nothing but darkness and stars around him, prompted him to a blunt honesty he usually tried to avoid. Staring at the sky, he reluctantly said, "I won't forget you either, Sammy. I think I couldn't even if I tried."

And once this was over...

He *would* try.

Chapter Fourteen

The next night, they lay in a real bed together, and Sam closed her eyes, perfectly content to be where she was, surrounded by Egyptian cotton and down pillows as fluffy as clouds, with Taylor's hard arms wrapped around her tightly. No matter how many hours she spent in his bed as he brought her to heights she'd never seen before, she still ached for one more time before walking away—something she was smart enough to know she should have done long ago, but not smart enough to actually do.

Even now, as she lay there, naked and coated in a thin sheen of sweat, completely satisfied and weak, she wanted nothing more than to whisper her secrets to him, to open up to him in ways she never had to anyone else.

It was as dangerous as it was unwelcome.

They'd spent the day as planned, building houses together, making the world a better place one piece of wood at a time, and another night at the soup kitchen before eating at Fado Irish Pub. It would be so easy to fall into a routine with him, to let herself come to expect and rely on these weekends together—not to mention the weeknights—but she couldn't fall into routines.

Not with *him*.

She should get up, dress herself, thank him for the fun time, and never return…before she did the unthinkable and actually fell for the guy. There were a million reasons why she couldn't do that—his job, his social status, his money, her past, their agreement, their mutual unwillingness to fall in love, just to name a few—and she hadn't forgotten a single one of them. As a matter of fact, they kept her awake at night, after his quiet, even breathing filled the night's silence.

And yet…

She didn't get up.

Didn't walk away.

She needed to get her head on straight and focus on what really mattered. Volunteering in every possible way. Working hard to succeed at her job, with late nights at the office instead of cutting out at five to rush back to Taylor. Her goals. Saving companies…

"You're being quiet," he said, his voice rumbling in his chest, where her ear rested. His hand ran down her back, absentmindedly rubbing her. "Everything okay?"

She ran a finger through his crisp chest hair, drawing a circle. "Yeah, just…thinking."

"Uh-oh," he teased, the smile he undoubtedly wore audible in his voice. "Watch out, world. She's thinking."

She smacked his chest playfully.

"What's on your mind, Sammy?"

Her shoulders stiffened at the nickname. Not because she didn't like it—because she *did*. It had seemed a fluke before, just a nickname pulled out while staring at the beauty of the stars, but he'd used it several times since. "Just some work stuff. I met with that client again, Mr. Harper—"

"Mr. Harper?" he asked, his tone tight.

"Yeah. And he's thinking about taking the offer some cutthroat asshole of a consolidator gave him." She tilted her head and offered him a slight smile. "No offense."

He flexed his jaw. "Maybe he's taking it because it's a good offer and it's his best option. There's a good chance he's tired of trying to save something that is impossible and he needs a way out. Have you ever thought about that?"

She lifted on an elbow, her heart picking up speed at his argumentative tone. She hadn't mentioned work since he'd gotten upset when she called him the enemy, but now that she'd opened up and talked to him, he was *angry*?

His anger spurred her own, and she clutched at it desperately.

"No, I haven't, because losing your dream is never a good thing." She pushed off his chest, tugging the sheet with her. If she was going to argue with him about whether he was doing something good by ending companies, it wouldn't be with her naked boobs (along with red chafing from his five o'clock shadow) hanging out.

He let his hand drift away from her back and sat up against the headboard, settling what was left of the sheet over his lap. "Maybe some dreams need to die, Sam."

"Maybe they don't need help getting there," she gritted out.

His nostrils flared. "Maybe they do and you just refuse to see it."

They stared at one another, breathing heavily.

She won the unspoken contest they'd been having, because he spoke first.

"I don't like the way you talk about my job, like it makes me a bad guy."

When she opened her mouth, he held a hand up, glowering at her. "I swear to God if you say it *does* make me a bad guy, I'll fucking explode."

She pressed her mouth into a thin line. "It doesn't make you a *bad guy*, but you basically swoop in when people are at the lowest point in their lives, when they're desperate for a solution—*any* solution—that makes sense, and you offer them an out that not only ends the very thing they're fighting for, but which, when everything is said and done, is tailored to make you a pretty profit and make your portfolio nicer. You're not looking out for them—you're in it for you."

"It's my *job* to take unprofitable companies and either make them profitable, and save some jobs in the process, or to know it's impossible to save a sinking ship, and to close it altogether," he said through gritted teeth. "I'm the guy who is best equipped to make that call."

"Why? Because you've become rich off of other people's failures?"

He shook his head. "No. Because I'm not too emotionally attached to the company to see what's dragging it down in the first place, and not too naive to think I can overcome it if I just *try* hard enough."

The way he said that last part, all high-pitched in a poor imitation of her voice, left no doubt in her mind he mocked her—which she might have found funny if rage wasn't pounding through her body.

She stood, ripping the sheet off the bed with her and wrapping it around her body—leaving him naked and vulnerable. "Or maybe you're so cold and dead inside that you're too quick to ignore the whole picture, and you don't even try to see a way to save the company before you rip it apart, bone by bone, and feed it to the dogs."

He got out of bed, his motions jerky. "Cold, huh?"

She wasn't sure if he referred to her current status and her hogging of the sheets, or her interpretation of his emotional status. Either way: "Yep."

"That's real funny, coming from you."

She hugged herself, holding the sheet in place. "I'm not cold. I try to save people. To help them. You—"

"Oh, I wasn't talking about your work," he snapped. "You're all about the warm and fuzzy shit there. Saving unicorns and building rainbows, or whatever the hell it is you do in your office that definitely doesn't include facing the realities of life and the fact that your clients are fucked before they ever step foot in your office."

She bit her tongue. "At least I'm not the frigging grim reaper—"

"I'm talking about here, with me, in this room," he continued, standing there completely naked and clearly perfectly content to do so.

How could she argue with him when that glorious body was on display?

Maybe that was part of his plan.

Distract her with his abs and win.

Not today, Satan.

"What we just did wasn't very cold," she argued. Bending down, she picked up the pants he'd removed earlier tonight and chucked them at him. "For God's sake, get dressed."

He cocked a brow at her, letting the clothing hit him in the chest and fall to the floor. "What we just did in that bed had nothing to do with emotions and everything to do with fucking for pleasure."

She recoiled. She couldn't help it. "You wouldn't know emotions if they punched you in the face," she countered.

He laughed. Icily. "You're going to call me out on my lack of emotions when you run every time I try to talk about anything you deem too personal to be questioned?"

"Considering you never let yourself trust me enough to let go of your control in bed, and never stop playing by your rules even when your head is between my thighs?" She flipped her hair over her shoulder. "Yeah, I am."

"Maybe when you stop clamming up when I ask you where you went to school, or what your favorite foods were as a kid, or where your parents live—maybe, *just maybe*, I'd consider letting you take control in the bed."

"Fine," she snapped. "While we're at it, why don't we talk about what it is that makes you so desperate to hold on to control over everything in your life in the first place."

He threw his hands up. "Sure, why not? Why don't I tell you every little detail about my life, from the time of my birth until now, and change everything about myself, from the foods I eat to the way I fuck, all because you want me to—but, hey, you don't have to change a damn thing about yourself or the way you keep me at a distance, because you're *just fine* the way you are."

She took a step toward him. "I'm not asking you to change. I told you, I'm not that girl. I'm simply saying you get mad at me for being closed off, and not liking your job—"

"Or my bank account."

"—but clearly you're just as closed off as me, as you should be. After all, like you said, we're just fucking in that bed, right?" she shot at him, ignoring his comment about his money. "This is all just one big first date."

"That's what we agreed on."

She nodded, swallowing hard. "So why does it bother you if I don't like your job?"

"I don't know," he answered, not meeting her eyes. "Why does it bother you that I fuck you the same way I did every other girl I brought into this bed, if you just want a good time?"

Just the idea of him lumping her in with every other woman he'd had sex with...ugh. It *hurt*. It shouldn't. But it *did*. "I..." She broke off, swallowing hard.

Something unwanted must have slipped into her expression.

He flinched, dragging a hand down his face. "I didn't mean—"

"Yeah, you did." She lifted her chin. "And that's fine. After all, that's all this is. Meaningless, fun, mindless pleasure. When it's over, I'm supposed to get dressed and leave, like the other girls do, but I've been staying. Speaking of which…" She glanced at her wrist. It was bare. "Wow. Look at the time, I should go. Busy day at the office tomorrow. Lots of unicorns to rescue."

He let out a moan and walked toward her. "Sammy—"

"Don't 'Sammy' me," she snapped, dropping her sheet and picking up her panties. "This conversation was enlightening. Truly. Just what I needed to get my head on straight."

He flexed his jaw, watching her dress. As she stepped into her pants, he asked, "What is that supposed to mean?"

"Nothing," she muttered.

"What a surprise, you won't let me in."

She stiffened, yanking her sweater over her head and leaving her bra on the floor. She needed to get out of here ASAP, before she did something stupid. That hollow ache in her chest, that burning sting in her eyes…it might have been a long time, but she was gonna cry.

Over *him*.

Stupid.

Grabbing her stuff, she shoved her bra into her purse and picked up her shoes, not bothering to take the time to shove her feet into them. Facing him, she squared her shoulders and forced a calm expression to her face that rivaled his stony countenance. "Hey, this was fun, but I think it's time we call it quits, huh? After all, people on their first date aren't supposed to care enough to fight like this, right?"

He paled, not moving, still as naked as he'd been when he'd brought her to pleasure minutes before. "You're walking away? Just like that?"

She met his eyes, refusing to let herself hurt because he wasn't even trying to stop her from leaving. Why should he? They were just having fun. There was no obligation for him to try to make her happy or to resolve their fight. She might as well continue to prop up an icy facade, to appear as cold as he seemed to think she was. As cold as *he* was.

She snapped her fingers. "Just like that."

And then she did it.

She *left*.

It wasn't until the elevator doors closed and she stepped into her sneakers, hopping on one foot while holding on to the metal bar on the wall and trying to keep her balance, that she dropped the act and let the tears fall down her face—tears she had *no* right shedding over a guy who didn't give a damn about her.

Stupid, *stupid* girl.

Chapter Fifteen

He shouldn't be here, shouldn't be doing this.

If she wanted to end things, fine. She had that right. They had agreed early on that their date could easily be terminated on either side and that neither one of them had any claims to the other when that moment came. He stood by that promise, since he was a man of his word.

What he *didn't* stand by was what he'd said that had caused her to leave him.

Comparing her to his past lovers had been wrong on so many levels, but her ripping apart everything he did and accusing him of being cold and dead inside had made the spark he'd been denying was inside him for the past week burst into a full-fledged combustion. He wasn't cold and dead, and he *did* know what emotions were, and it was *all* her damn fault.

She'd broken past every defense he had in place to guard his life and himself, and she'd had the audacity to tell him that he was the grim reaper come to life.

He *wasn't*. Not anymore.

Truth was, he never should have let himself get angry, or

let go of his self-control…one of the many things she didn't like about him. But look what happened when he did.

He said stupid shit that lost him the girl.

While there was probably no fixing that or going back in time to do things differently, he could fix the way she remembered him, at the very least. He could tell her the truth. And if that didn't change anything, so be it. He would give her what she wanted. But first…

Time to lose control one more time.

He lifted his hand, knocked three times, and waited, heart pounding, to find out whether or not she'd let him in. Rage boiled through him, and, at the same time, panic—that she might not open the door. Would she give him a chance to make things right?

After an indeterminable amount of torturous time, the lock slid against metal, and the door opened slightly, and her face appeared through the thin crack. "How did you find out my apartment number?"

He rested a sweaty palm on the wall next to her door. Since when did he get nervous? He brokered million-dollar deals without so much as a bead of sweat. "I told you, I own this place."

"I thought that was a joke, not for—" She cut herself off. "Never mind. Of course, it wasn't a joke. You probably never joke about money, huh?"

He shook his head slightly. "I won't apologize for having the foresight to buy this place when it was dirt cheap—or for keeping it open so people can live in it and I can make money off of it."

She crossed her arms.

He met her eyes. Hers were bloodshot and devoid of makeup. A little red, too. Had she been *crying*? "May I come in?" he asked hesitantly.

"Sure, why not? I mean, it's yours." She stepped aside, letting him in. He drank in the sight of her home greedily, searching for any hints of the woman behind the mask. "Don't mind the mess. I wasn't expecting company."

It wasn't a mess at all…unless the blanket on the couch counted as "messy." Her home was small, tidy, and personalized with flowers, pillows, a few books—and yet there wasn't a single personal item that wouldn't be in a model home. Just enough decorations to make it her style, along with a couch, a TV, a small dining room table with one chair, and a coffee table with a book on learning French lying in the middle. Oh, and a few cat toys in a basket in the corner.

Why was she learning French?

"Nice place," he said, stopping short of her couch.

She remained standing, too, keeping her distance. "What are you doing here?"

Well, time to get to it.

"I hold on to control over everything in my life because as a kid, the only thing I could control was myself. If I cried, my mom cried, and she was already so tired, so I decided at a very young age not to do that anymore. Not to lose control over myself…*ever*. I don't like the way it makes me feel, even now."

She shook her head. "You don't have to explain—"

"Yeah, I do."

She hugged herself tighter, nodding.

"I brought that same sense of self-control to the bedroom, once I was old enough, and I have never once been with a girl who threatened to make me lose the hold I have over myself in bed." He flexed his jaw. "Not once."

"I know," she said, lifting her tiny nose in the air. "You made that pretty clear earlier, so I don't know why you drove over here—"

"I had an Uber bring me, because I'm a little bit drunk." He held his fingers up and made a tiny crack between his thumb and pointer finger. "Enough to make it possible for me to say what I'm about to say, but not so much that my head's not on straight enough to make sure I don't fuck it up." He paused. "It's a very thin line between the two."

Her lips twitched into an almost-smile. It was the prettiest almost-smile he'd ever seen, because it gave him hope that all might not be lost. "I'm sure."

"What I'm trying to say here is that no one even threatened that hold I have over myself...until you." He took a step toward her. "The first time I took you to my bed, I lost control of myself. You threaten it every damn day without even trying, and that scares the shit out of me."

She hugged herself even tighter, standing her ground.

"I lied when I said I fucked you the same way I did every other woman. I lost it and said shit I didn't mean." He flexed his jaw. "Because of that, I lost you, which is ironic, considering you're the first woman I tried so damn hard to keep."

Her fingers dug into her pajama shirt—which had cats on it. Fucking *cats*.

Her hair was pulled in a loose ponytail, her eyes wide and so bright they were blinding. She took his breath away with her beauty. "Taylor..."

Not wanting her to stop him, he continued on in a rush. "I want to know more about you because whatever this is we have going on between us—call it what you want—but you're not meaningless, and this isn't just sex. You're more than that. You're my—friend. And I don't want to lose you. Not yet. Maybe not ever."

She shook her head.

"I care about whether you like me or not, and it kills me that you don't right now, because I like you so damn much. Enough to let go and put the ball in your court. Enough to break a lifetime habit and let you in even if you won't do the same for me. Please don't end our first date, Sammy. Not yet. I'm not ready."

Her lower lip trembled, and she bit it. "I...I don't know

what to say."

"Then don't say anything. Let me show you what I mean."

Hunger gnawed at him as he claimed her mouth, tasting her with abandon. Anger at his stupid mistakes plagued him, but as her mouth moved under his, all that was left was hope warming his chest.

Growling, he backed her against the wall, lifting her up. She moaned, wrapping her arms around his neck, and he made quick work of removing all obstacles of clothing as his mouth worked over hers impatiently. Sliding his hand in between them, he teased her core, playing with her until she clung to him, crying his name out.

And when she stiffened, her body grasping for the release he'd normally deny her until he decided it was time, he let her go, giving her what she wanted and not thinking twice. Collapsing against the wall, she waited as he rolled the condom on, her chest rising and falling rapidly.

Her cheeks were flushed, her hair a mess, her lips swollen. *I did that. She's mine.*

And he was hers.

As soon as he had a condom on, he slid between her thighs, moving in to kiss her but stopping moments shy of actually doing so, his cock at the point of entering her luscious body even though it still trembled from the pleasure he'd given her, but not actually burying himself inside her.

"This is just me. No calculated plans that I mapped out before I even touched you, no self-control holding me back. Just me taking you because if I don't have you one more time before you walk away, I might fucking die. Just you, me, and nothing in our way."

She nodded, letting out a shuddered breath. "*Do it.*"

Kissing her, he thrust inside with one hard stroke. She urged him on, digging her heels into his lower back, and he closed his eyes, letting himself enjoy her body wrapped around his, his body deep inside hers. Each thrust took a piece of himself he would never see again and gave it to her, and he could only hope she would hold on to it tightly.

As tightly as she held him now.

His mouth softened on hers as he deepened his motions, burying his hand in her hair as he cradled the back of her head. She cried out his name into his mouth, her body quivering as she squeezed him, bringing him closer until he moved inside her with an abandon he'd never experienced before.

Just like he'd promised, he let go of everything and lost himself in her arms. He'd never been so goddamn *free* before.

With one last stroke, he came explosively, and she was right there with him, arching her back with bite marks on her neck that he didn't remember putting there. Letting out a breath, he dropped his head on the cool wall, supporting her weight as he came back down from the high she'd sent him on.

Pulling back, he examined her face for a sign of, well, anything, running his thumbs over her cheeks. Her eyes were closed. "Sam…?"

She opened her lids, those crystal-blue depths pulling him under. He didn't bother to fight it. There was no use. He was already drowning, and nothing would save him. "Yeah?"

"Would you like me to leave now, alone? Or…" He cut off, his voice raw and his emotions even rawer. He was wide open for her. Vulnerable. Exposed. "…or do you want to come home with me?"

Touching his cheek with an open palm, she ran her fingers over his stubble, offering him a small smile. Her cheeks were pink, her hair a mess, her lips swollen. She was everything he'd never known he wanted—no, *needed*. With one simple sentence, she saved him from himself. "I want you to take me home."

Chapter Sixteen

"And you went back to his place?" Izzy asked, sipping her coffee.

Sam's best friend had returned from Vegas a different woman and had yet to tell her the whole story of what had gone down out there. Her long blond hair fell over her shoulders, at direct contrast with her deep brown eyes. She wore fingerless mittens and a matching slouchy hat she'd probably knitted.

Sam nodded.

"And because of this…" Izzy frowned. "You guys are still on your first date?"

"Yep. As long as I keep sleeping at his place every night, we're still on our first date, so we have to keep coming back together to finish it out properly," Sam said, smiling.

Izzy, though, seemed less impressed. "So, he doesn't want a second date? And that doesn't…upset you?"

"No," she answered as honestly as she could, trying not to show that she shared her friend's doubt. "Why would it? I don't want more than a temporary thing, either. Plus, he's got a lot of rules and patterns… He doesn't like change."

When said out loud, it made him sound like a bore.

But he was so much more. He'd fought for her and stole her breath with every smile, sigh, and touch. He was the man who broke his rules for her and who wasn't pushing her to do the same.

"He sounds like an old man."

Sam sighed. "He's not. He's…"

Wonderful. Amazing. Handsome. Breathtaking.

After a period of silence, Izzy whistled through her teeth. "Wow."

"What?" she asked, ripping herself out of her mind and abandoning her search for the perfect adjective to describe an indescribable man like Taylor.

"You." Her best friend gestured at her, pursing her lips. "You've got it *bad*."

Sam's cheeks heated. "No, I don't."

"Girls who drift off with that dreamy look in their eyes when talking about a guy always have it bad." She sat back, folding her arms. "You can thank me for that."

Sam winced. "I'm sorry, by the way, about that whole mix-up. And for how your trip to Vegas turned out."

"At least I found out he was a lying, cheating son of a bitch before I married him, right?" Izzy asked, her face emotionless but her eyes telling a whole other story.

She reached out and touched her best friend's hand. "Izzy—"

"It's fine. I'm fine."

Sam didn't argue.

Izzy sighed. "Apparently Andrew really liked the woman who bought him for the night, too." She grinned. "I'm a regular old fairy godmother, only instead of finding princes who probably couldn't find a G-spot with a magnifying glass and a map, I'm setting people up with amazing sex with my *bippity, boppity, boo* crap."

Sam choked on a laugh. "You realize you just said your brother is good in bed, right?"

"Ew, gross." She tossed her hair over her shoulder. Half the guys in the room sighed. "Though, he's related to me, so he'd have to be. Good sex runs in the blood."

Sam shook her head. "Where did you go last night? Sorry I couldn't come along."

Her best friend gazed out the window. "It's fine. I actually liked being alone. I went to a book reading, and the woman had an amazing voice. She made me want to write again."

"Really?" Sam asked, smiling. Izzy used to write all the time, back in college, but it had been a long time since she let herself enjoy that passion, since teaching took up most of her time. "What do you want to write?"

"I don't know," she answered honestly. "But I opened a blank document yesterday, and some words just kinda fell out onto the page. So far, all I know is that my main character is a detective, and she's trying to find a killer who's terrifying a small town."

"So...a mystery?"

"Maybe." Diane shrugged. "I named the killer Tom."

Her ex-fiancé's name. "Is he going to die at the end?"

"I hope so."

Sam laughed, tracing an invisible path on the gray tabletop. "I'll go with you to the next reading. I'd like to see what it's like."

Izzy grinned. "Maybe by then, your 'date' will be over."

"Maybe..."

"Tell me more about him," Izzy said.

Sam shook her head. "The last thing you want to hear about is my love life. Let's talk about your book—"

"No. I want distractions. I want to hear all about your love life in excruciating detail. Go."

"Fine..." Sam hesitated. "Last night, he told me I was the

first girl to threaten his self-control and that I'm more than a lover—I'm his friend. It was nice and all, but we don't make sense."

"Why not?" Izzy asked, frowning.

"Because he's rich, for starters."

Izzy shook her head. "That doesn't put him in the same category as your parents, it just makes him a smart businessman."

"I know that, but I don't want to be rich, or have Egyptian cotton sheets and heated bathroom floors, and I refuse to take anything for granted."

Izzy shrugged. "Then don't."

"But he also moves in the same circles my parents did," Sam argued. "People would realize who I was, eventually, and rip him apart for being associated with my family."

"If he's willing to take that risk, let him."

"I can't say whether he is or not, since he doesn't know anything about my past." Sam took a sip of coffee. Izzy was the only one who knew the full story about her life and what she'd been through. She'd never told another soul and probably never would.

Even though they were out of jail and had been for three years now, she had no intention of seeing them. Ever.

"But—" Izzy started.

"No," Sam cut in. "No buts. He's fun, and I like him, and he's good in bed, but we have an agreement to keep things as-is, and I intend to hold him to it."

"If you say so," Izzy said, holding her hands up in surrender. "But if you ask me, it sounds like he wants more than that."

Sam avoided her eyes. "He was just saying nice things because we got in a fight."

"Or because he cares and wants more," Izzy argued. "And judging by the fact that you're continuing to hang with him against your better judgment, I'm going to guess that you do, too."

"No, I don't, because that would be stupid, and I'm not dumb."

Izzy snorted. "Keep telling yourself that."

She sipped her coffee, actively avoiding her friend's gaze, and stumbled upon something she couldn't believe. It was as if she'd magically conjured him by speaking about him. She blinked, doubting her vision, but sure enough, he stood outside the coffee shop, holding a briefcase and wearing the same long gray wool coat he'd left the apartment in this morning. The collar was upturned to protect him from Chicago's biting wind, and his hair was mussed.

"That's him," she hissed, kicking Izzy under the table. "Out there."

Izzy's eyes widened. When she gasped, Sam grinned. "The guy in the *Sherlock*-esque jacket?"

"Mmhm."

"I didn't think anyone else could rock an upturned collar besides Benedict Cumberbatch, but *damn*." She turned back to Sam, snapping her fingers. "If you're not willing to risk it all for a guy who looks like that, you don't deserve amazing sex. I take my gift back."

Sam laughed. "You can't do that."

"Sure, I can. I'm magic, bitch."

He had his back to her, so he hadn't seen her. Watching him without his knowledge was wrong, but she was way too curious about what he was up to outside of the office to care too much.

"I wonder who he's meeting," Izzy said.

Sam stiffened, her mind going in a million different directions all at once. "What makes you think he's meeting someone?"

"Why else would he hang outside in the cold when he

could be in here where the coffee and heat is?" she asked. "Are you going to say hi to him or lower your head, wait to see if he sees you, and act surprised when he does, as if you didn't see him coming from a mile away?"

Sam pursed her lips. "I'm gonna go with option B."

"Then lower your head. He's coming in with a girl—oh, she's pretty."

"What?" Sam snapped, lifting her head.

Sure enough, a gorgeous woman stood beside him, talking animatedly. He offered her an indulgent smile, and his eyes held a warmth that she thought had been reserved for her.

How silly of her.

"Maybe she's a work colleague? Or a client?" Sam whispered.

Izzy nodded. "I'm sure."

"It doesn't mean anything—" Sam broke off.

Why?

Because the woman *reached* out and *picked* a fuzzy off his jacket, and he didn't react *at all*. It was as if she did it all the time and had every right to touch him like that.

Who *was* she?

"That's…SAM. She picked *lint* off him."

Sam lowered her head, her heart twisting painfully. "I saw."

"No one does that, except…"

Except people who were close. Like boyfriend/girlfriend close.

Why was this girl touching him like that?

"I know." Jealousy and a deeper, sharper emotion which could only be called pain struck her heart. She stood, grabbing her coat with a trembling hand. "Let's go, quick, before he sees me."

Izzy grabbed her stuff, shooting a scowl at Taylor's

unknowing back. "Asshole."

Sam swallowed, not bothering to defend him. As they made their way to the door, Sam's heart sped up at the deep timbre of his voice. She was close to him. Too close.

"—and I told him to close the deal as soon as possible. The quicker we liquidate the assets and hit that bottom line, the quicker the pain will be over. I'm in line to make a lot of money off this one."

The woman grinned. "Good job."

Sam rolled her hands into fists.

Taylor and the mystery woman moved another step forward, still talking about the money about to hit his account. The woman laughed, patting him on the back as she spoke.

Green. Pure green.

That was *her* back. *Her* man.

Izzy tugged her sleeve. "Come on."

"Yeah, okay." She tore her eyes off them, heading for the door. "Let's go."

They almost made it when:

"Sam?" his voice called.

She stiffened, torn between pretending not to hear him and turning around.

"Hey, Sam!" he called even louder.

Izzy mouthed, "Oh, shit."

Plastering a smile on her face, she spun. "Taylor. Hey."

Her gaze slid past him to the woman who held a cup of coffee in her left hand. She had an engagement ring on her finger—a huge frigging diamond.

Oh God, she was going to be sick.

All over his shiny leather shoes.

"What are you doing here?" he asked.

He didn't introduce her to his friend. "Having coffee with Izzy." She gestured to Izzy, who waved but didn't smile. "You?"

"Having coffee, too," he said, watching as his companion sat at the table they'd just left.

She forced the smile to remain. "I guess Monday is coffee day, huh?"

"Yeah." He cocked a brow. "You okay?"

She nodded.

"Okay…" He glanced over his shoulder to the awaiting brunette. "Well, I should go. See you tonight at eight?"

She held her smile in place. "We're still on?"

"Yeah, why wouldn't we be?" he asked slowly, running his fingers through his hair.

She shrugged.

He smiled at Izzy. "It was nice meeting you."

Izzy tipped her head, still not smiling.

He walked off and sat with his companion. He was close enough for Sam to hear his date ask, "Who is she?"

Taylor shrugged. "A…friend. Hey, are we still going to that fundraiser at the museum Friday night?"

The brunette nodded.

"Okay, I'll make arrangements for a car to pick us up," he said, pulling his phone out.

Sam didn't stick around to hear another word. She pushed through the doors, the lump in her throat threatening to cut off her oxygen. He'd secured a night out with another woman, right after making sure she was coming to his place later that night?

This didn't seem like something Taylor would do.

There *had* to be a logical explanation to this.

Taylor might not be the relationship type of guy, but she hadn't taken him for a more-than-one-woman-at-a-time kind of guy. So that woman…who was she?

And why did Sam have an invisible spike lodged in her chest?

Chapter Seventeen

Later that night, Taylor paced the length of his living room, checking the clock impatiently. It was half past eight, and Sam had been scheduled to show up at his place at eight.

Where the hell was she?

He hated tardiness and veering off schedule.

To be honest, though, she'd acted weird when they ran into one another at Starbucks, but he'd written it off as her just being surprised to see him outside of their prearranged times and had told himself that maybe she hadn't liked him saying hello to her in front of her friend. Or maybe it was something else altogether, and he was reading too much into that one encounter.

But if so, *what*?

"Sir?" his secretary said through the phone.

He tightened his grip on his iPhone. "Yeah?"

"Should we go ahead with pressing Mr. Harper for an answer? We've given him the allotted waiting period."

He hesitated, thinking of Sam.

There was no doubt that she was determined to save

Harper Enterprises, but the thing was, they were too out of touch with current technological advances. The most they could hope for was a peaceful death of the company and a generous buyout—something *Taylor* could give them.

But with Sam trying to work the case from the other angle, not knowing he was the buyer she was fighting, there was no denying his reluctance to pull the trigger. If he closed the company she was working so hard to save, it might be the end of them. But if he didn't close the deal, hundreds of jobs would be lost.

At least with his offer, *some* of those jobs would be saved.

It was his duty to push for acceptance, after the appropriate waiting period passed. That time had come and gone, so he had to follow up with Mr. Harper and show him why closing the business was his best option, no matter how painful that realization might be. In the end, Mr. Harper would agree, he just needed help getting there. That was where Taylor came in.

Still, he hesitated.

"Schedule a dinner for Monday of next week. Give him some more time to think over all his options," he said. Even as the words left his mouth, they were the wrong ones.

The longer he waited, the less likely they would be to reach an optimum solution. If he didn't save the company, and if Sam didn't come up with a solution, a lot of people might suffer because of his reluctance to piss off his lover.

But what if she was right?

What if she could save Mr. Harper?

"All right," his secretary said. "I'll write it down…if I can find a pen. I swear I had one on my desk earlier. *Where* do they keep going?"

Taylor winced. "I may have grabbed it off your desk earlier. I'm sorry." The elevator door opened behind him. His heart leapt because it could only be one person. Sam was the only person who had the clearance from security to come directly up without a phone call. "I have to go."

"Wait. About the benefit Friday night—"

"I have it covered. I'm going with Julie." He hung up, turning on Sam. "You're late."

She crossed her arms over her chest, not removing her coat or purse. "That's because I almost didn't come."

So. Something *was* up.

His stomach fisted, and he moved toward her, examining her for a hint of what was going on in her mind. Had she found out about his direct role in the dissolution of Harper Enterprises? "Why not?"

"Because…" She bit her lip, adjusting her weight. She was clearly struggling to find the words to say what she needed to say. Well, shit, this was it. She was going to end it with him. "Who is Julie?"

He blinked. Out of all the things he expected her to say, that was not it. "Julie?"

"Yeah. Is she the woman you were with today?"

Just like that, her behavior made perfect sense. It hadn't even occurred to him that she might be uncertain about his companion, because he never had anyone who gave a damn who he was with or why. But to Sam, it had probably looked a hell of a lot like a date. "Sam—"

"At first, I thought she might be a girlfriend, but she had a ring on her finger, and unless you lied about not being the relationship type, you definitely didn't put it there."

He wasn't sure what to say. Apparently, she didn't put it past him to *cheat* on a girlfriend with her, but the ring on her finger was out of the question.

"And I thought maybe she's your sister, but she didn't act like a sister. She was too touchy-feely, and to be honest, the way she touched you…it made me jealous. Was she your sister? Am I wrong?"

The fact that she was jealous…he wasn't going to lie. He liked that she cared enough to succumb to the little green monster. She might not have said the actual words last night, like he had, but if she'd gotten jealous over him, clearly there was *something* there, right? "She's not my sister."

She stopped unbuttoning her jacket. "Oh."

"But she's not my fiancée, either." After a second, he added, "Or my girlfriend. She's just a friend, a good one."

She stared.

"Her fiancé is a Marine, and he's on tour overseas, so we go to social events together. We have a ball Friday night, and if I remember correctly, I'm not allowed to ask you to go to society events with me due to some mysterious reason."

She swallowed, her hands still frozen on her third button.

He closed the distance between them, gently pushing her hands away to finish the task. She let him, still not speaking. "We're just friends, Sam. I'm all yours until you don't want me anymore."

Cupping his cheeks, she rose on tiptoe, locking eyes with him. He held on to her jacket, his heart thumping against his ribs in a quick staccato. "I…I don't know what we are, what to call us, because we can never be together, not for real. But the idea of you being with someone else? I don't like it."

"Why can't we ever be together, Sam?" he asked quietly, knowing he was pushing his luck but too damn curious to really care. She kept saying that they couldn't be together, and he needed to know why. Had she killed someone? Gone to jail? Escaped?

Why couldn't they be together?

"You don't want to be with me," she argued, going paler than the vampires in that movie where instead of being killers, they sparkled in the sun.

He shrugged. "But if I did? Why would that be so horrible?"

He wasn't saying he *wanted* that or anything, but *why*?

"Because I can't." She bit her lip. "I wouldn't do that to you."

He blinked. "I don't under—"

"What I'm trying to say is that being with you is special to me. When this is all said and done and our date is over, I'd like to remain friends, because I don't want to lose you, Taylor."

What did she mean when she said she wouldn't *do that to him*? He opened his mouth to ask, but then her mouth was on his and she was undoing his shirt. There weren't supposed to be any long-term feelings, but damn it, he wanted more. She needed to be *his*, and he wouldn't accept anything less.

She dropped to her knees, and his heart choked him as she undid his pants. Usually he was the one to drive his lovers insane with his mouth, his tongue, his touch. "Sam—"

"Shh." His pants hit the floor. "Let me do this. I want to do it."

Red lips moved closer to his cock, and his fingers buried themselves in her soft hair. She spun her tongue in circles as she sucked, locking his gaze on her as his lids lowered in pleasure. This blowjob was unlike anything he'd ever experienced before. Every stroke of her tongue, every caress of her fingertips across his bare skin, took part of him away that he'd never given to anyone else, and probably never would again. Sam took him…and gave him nothing in return.

He wasn't so sure he liked that…

But he sure as hell liked her mouth on him.

Moaning, she moved closer, cupping his shaft as she moved her mouth over him, driving him to ecstasy. When she deepened the strokes, sucking harder, he stiffened, his entire body straining toward release. His balls pulled tight, his stomach clenched, and her mouth worked some kind of magic on him—the kind he hadn't really believed existed until her.

"Sam, I'm—"

She nodded, sucking harder, and pushed closer to him, refusing to budge.

He groaned, the sight of her on her knees fucking him with her mouth killing any tiny hold he had on himself. With a thrust of his hips, he came, seeing stars.

That's right. Motherfucking *stars*.

She sat back, swiping her hand over her lips.

"Jesus," he growled.

"Nope, just me," she said, repeating his phrase from their first date. She stood, wobbling on her feet a little. "I like— *agh*."

He flattened her on the couch, crawling on top of her, effectively cutting her off with a kiss. After tasting himself on her tongue, he pulled back, locking eyes with her. "I've given you so much of me, shit I've never given anyone else, so I'm breaking my word. I'm demanding more of you than you're willing to give. I want you—no, I *need* you to be mine." His hand slid between her legs, touching her core. "If you can't give that to me, if I can't call you mine even for a short time, I don't want to do this anymore."

She sucked in a breath. "Taylor..."

"I'm serious. I want to be your boyfriend."

Her increased breathing rate was the only sign of life she gave. She remained perfectly still otherwise.

"Let's give this thing a name. Let's call it what it is: a fucking relationship. And no matter how short or long it is, you're mine, and I'm yours, and when we introduce each other to other people, that's what we say, instead of avoiding it since we don't know what to call each other without insulting each other."

She choked on a laugh. "You were confused today, too?"

"Yes, why do you think I didn't introduce you to Julie?"

She stopped laughing. "Because you didn't want to."

"I want to shout it from the rooftops—tell everyone you're mine. Let me, even if only for a little while."

She fell silent, debating her answer. He could see the wheels turning in her head. Whatever it was that held her back from him, clearly it was huge.

"Okay," she said quietly.

He stiffened. "Okay?"

She nodded. "Yes, I'll be your girlfriend."

Grinning, he kissed her, finally giving her what she wanted—himself.

Chapter Eighteen

The past couple of days with Taylor had been...there was no other word for it. Though she rarely used it, she had to make an exception this time. It had been *perfect*. He'd been so openly honest with her, and little by little, Sam was doing the same.

She'd told him she used to live in a mansion and had her every whim catered to and all about her childhood, including how she'd gone to prep school and moved up here to Chicago to not only go to college, but to escape her old life and all the trappings that came with it. Of course, she didn't mention what she was escaping, or what her parents had done, but that wasn't something she just told *anyone*.

Still, though, she wanted to tell him.

Maybe it was time.

But what if he called it all off?

Was she ready to take that risk?

She gripped her napkin, twisting it.

Empty dishes sat between them, since they'd just finished eating, and he'd filled their glasses with wine. It was Thursday night, which meant tomorrow night he'd have to leave her alone for a little while, since she still refused to accompany him to his charity gala, despite his repeated attempts at changing her mind.

Last night as they lay in bed together, he'd told her about his younger sister, Grace, and how she was pursuing her medical degree, almost finished with med school, and that he was paying for it in full. He also paid for his "little brother" to go to private school, so he could have his best shot at life. She was in awe of his generosity and kind heart.

He smiled at her, and she grinned back. "Did you change your mind yet?"

The grin faded away immediately. "No."

"But I don't understand why we can't go together. No one even knows who you are."

She made an impulsive decision to come clean. It was time for him to know who she was and what her parents had done. It was time to tell him the truth.

And if he didn't like her...

Then so be it. Or so she kept telling herself, anyway.

"I don't have any siblings."

He blinked at the abrupt change of topic but immediately adjusted, leaning forward eagerly. "Okay."

"As a kid, my parents were the best you could ask for. Anything I wanted? I got it. I was the apple of their eye. Their whole life. They never missed anything I did and came to every horrible concert, play, and game—whatever I was into at the time. They were there."

He nodded.

"Back then I thought the world revolved around them." She swallowed, admitting something for the first time. "I miss them, that version of them. They were all I had."

He picked up his wine, took a sip, and asked: "Have you ever thought about contacting them again?"

"I have thought about it." She picked up her wine, taking a big gulp. "My mom called me today to say happy birthday."

He slammed the glass down. "Wait. Hold up. It's your birthday?"

"Yeah." She waved a hand. "That's not the point."

He stood. "But—"

"The point I'm trying to make is that for the last ten years, one or both of them have called me on my birthday, and for the last ten years, I've ignored the call." She cleared her throat. "Until today. Today...I answered."

He sat back down, forehead still wrinkled over the fact that it was her birthday and she hadn't told him. Who cared, though, really? Birthdays stopped being fun once you were an adult. "And? How'd it go?"

"Horrible. She cried. I cried. She kept apologizing for what she'd done, and I..." She ran her hands down her face. "I almost wanted to tell her that it was okay. That I understood. That I was okay."

He reached out, caught her hand, and held on to it tightly. "And are you okay?"

The bright green of his eyes drew her in, making her a little less shaky. But if she was going to do this...if she was going to tell him what they'd done...she could lose him.

This might be the *end*.

Was she ready?

She nodded. "I am, because of you. I didn't realize it, but I was lonely before I met you. Being with you this past week and a half—"

"Is that all it's been?" he asked in surprise.

"—has shown me that I shouldn't have closed myself off to the world like I did. I shouldn't have avoided"—she gestured between them—"this. What we have. For the first time in years, I'm happy, and it's because of you, Taylor. You've made me happy."

He tightened his grip on her hand. "I'm happy, too."

"You are?" she asked, the words hard to get out past the giant lump in her throat.

"I am." He stood and pulled her to her feet. "You showed me that relationships aren't stupid after all. I always refused to budge from my plan, but being with you has shown me differently. Being with someone isn't all that bad, if you're with the right person."

The problem was, she wasn't the right person.

Not for him.

Yet, against all reason, against all odds, she wanted to be his happy ending. She wanted this to be real *forever*. Which meant... Oh God, she'd gone and done it.

She'd fallen in love with him.

Why else would she be dying to tell him how happy he made her, how she fell asleep smiling in his arms every night instead of hugging her pillow alone in the dark with tears under her cheek? Why else would she want to tell him the truth about her and let him decide whether or not she was worth the risk? Why else would she want to open herself up to that kind of rejection and pain, when he rightfully and inevitably said no?

Because she loved him.

And she wanted him to love her, too.

All of her.

She rose up on her tiptoes and kissed him.

When they were done, he kissed the top of her head.

There was something in that gesture, in the innocence of it, which stabbed her straight through her heart, something that should have hurt but instead made her...*whole.*

Her throat threatened to close up on her when he kissed the spot between her eyes, tightening his hold on her. Then he held her and gave her what she needed right now: him.

"Happy birthday, Sammy."

She buried her nose in his sweater and inhaled his scent deeply. "I'm sorry. I'm an emotional mess today. It's just with this, and work today...*ugh*."

He tilted her face up to his. The warmth shining in those green depths stole another piece of herself she'd been trying to keep. "You're beautiful, and compassionate, and funny, and smart. Not a mess. Never a mess."

She shook her head, stepping back. "How do you always say the right things?"

"I don't know." A frown creased his brow. "Are you okay? What happened today?"

"I'll tell you all about it," she said, taking a deep breath. She had to do it. Couldn't have this shoe hanging over her head for all eternity, about to drop. If she was going to be with him, she had to be honest, whether she liked it or not. "Everything, though you already know some of it."

He handed her the glass of wine, his face falling. "Oh... Is this about Mr. Harper?"

"Mr. Harper?" She blinked. "How do you know Mr. Harper?"

He frowned. "Your client? When we spoke earlier, I told him to go talk to you again, to look into—"

Oh, God. He was the man who was trying to consolidate Mr. Harper's company. He was the shark, waiting for there to be enough blood in the water to find his victim.

She should've *known*.

"I'm giving him more time so he can fully consider all his options," Taylor said quickly. "I backed off to give you time to come up with a solution...if you can."

Anger was there, hiding beneath all her self-doubt about her pending confession, but she tried to quell it before it took over. If they were going to do this—be *together*—they'd have to find a way to be on opposite sides of the table, both figuratively and metaphorically.

They had to make this work.

"Are you mad at me?" he asked so quietly she almost didn't hear it. "I should have told you I was the guy trying to buy the company, but I didn't want to ruin—"

She cupped his cheeks, shaking her head. "I'm not mad."

"You're…not?" he asked with surprise clear in his voice.

A smile escaped her. "Nope. We're going to have to learn how to lose graciously and win even more graciously against each other, without getting mad…right?"

"Right." He cradled the back of her head, his thumb on the bottom of her jawline. The way he looked at her… all warmth and desire, as if he would move anything to be with her, to help her, to be her man…it was why she couldn't quit him. "You never cease to amaze me. Every time I think you've finally finished, you surprise me with something else."

Her heart skipped a beat for more reasons than one.

He lowered his mouth, seeking hers.

This was it. It was time to let him decide for himself whether he wanted to be with the daughter of a couple who had stolen the dreams of thousands of people, or whether he wanted to walk away. This was the moment to open herself up to him, as he'd done to her. After she did so, after she came clean, there would be nothing standing in the way.

They could be together.

If he chose her.

But first…

"We need to talk." She backed out of his arms, knowing if she kissed him that she'd lose her nerve to tell him the truth about her past. But she needed just a *second* alone to come to terms with it all, to wrap her head around it, before she dove right in. "Can you give me a second?"

"Of course," he agreed, looking more nervous than before.

She needed a second to pull her nerve together, and a

little distance between them would help with that. As she headed for the bathroom, her heart pounded because oh my God, she was going to do this. Going to tell him the truth. She was actually—

As she passed his desk, something in the trash caught her eye. It wasn't the giant yellow envelope, or the logo of a private investigator plastered in the corner, either, though both of those were pretty attention-grabbing. It was her last name, barely noticeable, on a corner of a page sticking out of the envelope.

No. He didn't…he wouldn't…

Slowly, she bent and picked up the envelope, her heart twisting. Turning on her heel, she held it up. If she had any doubts as to what it was, they disappeared the second Taylor's face paled and his eyes widened. "What the hell is this?"

Chapter Nineteen

For over a week now, more than a whole damn week, he'd carried that *stupidly* requested report in his briefcase, not touching the damn thing, even going so far as to forget he'd put it in his briefcase in the first place. Of course, the day he remembered to get rid of it, to throw the thing out, she *had* to see it. He'd tossed it in the trash this morning before work, knowing his cleaning lady would be coming today, but she hadn't emptied the bin by his desk.

Why hadn't she emptied the fucking trash?

And why hadn't he tossed it at work, or shredded it?

Damn it.

Holding his hands up, he approached her slowly, not moving as fast as his mind was. "I can explain."

She shook the envelope. "Tell me this isn't what I think it is. Tell me you didn't hire someone to investigate me."

"In all fairness." He took another step toward her. "I ordered that report right after I met you, but—"

She slapped it on her thigh. "Oh, well, then, I guess you're forgiven."

"Really?" he asked suspiciously. After their earlier conversation and her forgiveness over the fact that he was the one who was trying to consolidate Mr. Harper's business, this was too easy.

She pressed her mouth into a thin line, trembling. "*No, not really.*"

Yep, too easy.

She looked seconds from killing him or walking away from him for good this time…maybe both. His chest tightened. *No.* She couldn't.

"I'm sor—"

"You know, I was finally beginning to actually *trust* you." She glared at the envelope, her shoulders stiff. "I was going to tell you everything, but you had to go and read it yourself. Did you like what you saw? I bet you laughed when you read about how I had to go live with foster parents when my real parents got arrested. Oh, and there's the part where I cried as the feds dragged my parents away in handcuffs and I was left all alone. That's a doozie, full of drama."

Wait. What?

Her *parents* had gone to *prison*?

"It's funny how they embezzled money from their employees, right?" She laughed, but it wasn't a laugh. "That was your favorite part, I bet."

"Embezzled…?" he said slowly, his mind reeling. "Your parents stole money? Went to prison?"

"Don't act like you didn't know," she snapped, shaking the file. "What was your favorite part? When I ran away from my foster home, and they forced me to go back? When I tried to live on the streets but only lasted four hours because I was too spoiled?"

She was telling him things he'd been desperate to hear, but now that she was telling him all this stuff, he was desperate to shut her up before she said too much.

This wasn't the way he'd wanted to find out.

"Sam, don't—" He held his hands out in a peace gesture.

"You know what? This is good." She nodded and scrunched her face up. "I'm glad you got all the dirty details like this. It only goes to show me that I was right about you the moment I saw you on that stage and judged you as an asshole who would do anything to win." She tossed the file on his desk. "Guess I was your opponent this time, and you won. How's it feel?"

He swallowed. "I didn't win, and I didn't read the file."

"It's open," she scoffed.

"Because I opened it but decided not to read." He held his hands out, imploring her to believe him. If she didn't, he'd lose her. He had to *fix* this. "I opened it when I got it, last Monday, and I never touched it again until today when I threw it away."

She hugged herself, face pale. "And I'm just supposed to, what, believe you? Take your word for it? *Trust* you?"

Something invisible squeezed his heart mercilessly. "Sam—"

"And even if you didn't read it, even if you're telling the truth, it doesn't matter." She slapped her palm with her clenched fist, no longer pale but red with anger. "None of this matters because we never should have let things get this far in the first place. You know that now, after reading the file. You know how wrong I am for you."

He hung his head, fisting his hands at his sides. "I didn't—"

"Don't deny it again."

Staring blankly at her, he wisely kept his mouth shut.

Sure, he could make up excuses, but he'd known ordering that report had been wrong, which was why he hadn't read it in the first place.

Why had he ordered that stupid report?

Her chest rose and fell rapidly, and she stood her ground,

not moving.

Every muscle in his body ached.

Now was not the time to get emotional, to lose control. A calm, clear head was necessary, and he needed to fix this fuck-up before she walked out the door.

"Are you going to say anything? Or are you just going to stand there, staring at nothing?"

"What can I say?" He gritted his teeth. "You're pissed at me, and you have every right to be. You're betrayed, and it's my fault. I could be a guy and make excuses and try to make you forgive me, but we both know I fucked up, and I'm sorry. I'll stand here and let you yell at me, and I'll take it, because I deserve it, but once you're done, I'll do my best to make it up to you. And make no mistake, Sam—I *will* make this up to you."

"I don't want you to," she growled.

He inclined his head. "But I will. I'm not going to lose you or let you push me away. Not after how far we've come."

"You already lost me, and you don't get to tell me whether I can leave or not," she rasped, biting her lip. "You shouldn't have ordered that report."

"I know, that's why I never read it."

She crossed her arms. "Allegedly."

"I didn't read it, and I won't."

He'd been nothing but honest with her, while she'd been hiding all sorts of shit about her past, and in *this* she refused to believe him. He tried not to let it bother him, since he was in the wrong here, but it did.

"Let me do it for you." She picked it up, advancing on him. "My parents stole millions of dollars from their company, from people who *trusted* them, robbing their employees of their retirement funds, and stocks, and 401(k)s so horribly that a company like yours had to take control, lay off hundreds of jobs, and ruin lives. On top of that, as if that wasn't enough, they also stole from the charity they'd created to help orphaned children—ironic, since through their actions, I became one."

His chest tightened. "You don't have to do this."

"Clearly, I do." She slapped him on the chest with the envelope. He kept his hands at his sides, refusing to take it. "You want to know so badly you paid someone to do the digging around for you, and he did it in such a timely manner, too. I mean, he had this report finalized two days after we met? That's impressive."

He stared straight ahead, focusing on the window. The city lights. Anything but her, because if he saw the pain and accusation in her eyes, he might lose the tiny grasp on his self-control he still clutched. "He's good at what he does."

"I'm sure he is." She tossed it on the couch, since he didn't take it. "It couldn't have been easy for him. I changed my last name and had the records sealed."

"You did?" he asked, trying to keep his tone flat.

She had a different last name. Jesus.

"Yeah, because I wanted a fresh start, I wanted a life where no one knew who my parents were or what they'd done." She pushed her hair out of her face, more than likely blinking rapidly in an attempt to hold back tears. "I didn't want people to know my shame."

She might as well have punched him in the gut with a spiked fist. He couldn't breathe. Couldn't move. Couldn't... "It's not your fault, and it's not your shame," he said, breaking his rule and looking at her. He shouldn't have, because he'd been right. It *killed* him. "You didn't steal that money. They did."

"I spent it, though. God, did I spend it."

He reached for her hand. "You didn't know."

"It doesn't matter," she snapped, slipping out of his reach. His hand was so damn empty without hers inside it. He fisted it, digging his fingers into his palm until it hurt. "Sins of the father, and all that. I might have been a kid, and I might not have known where all that money came from, but I will always be guilty by association. I will always be judged for what they did."

"Not by me," he said, his voice cracking. "Never by me."

"But by everyone else." She swallowed hard, for the first time losing the shield of anger she'd been clinging to, and what could only be described as fear was in her eyes. "Could you walk into a room of your peers, with me, the daughter of two federally convicted embezzlers, on your arm?"

He frowned. "I wouldn't give a damn."

"Not even when I'm judged as guilty, and you are, too, by association?"

He opened his mouth, closed it.

Bad public opinion could be catastrophic to his company.

Damn it, he'd worked hard to get where he was, and he had done so by keeping his hands and his nose clean. To be attached to a family that had done the complete opposite…

What would it do to him?

"Exactly," she said, tears welling in her eyes.

"No one would know who you were," he hurried to assure her, his words as hollow as his heart, because they weren't enough.

"Yeah, because it was so hard for you to figure it out," she shot back.

Swallowing, he tried to reach for her hand again. "We don't even know what he found out. For all we know there's nothing of your past in there."

Again, she jumped out of his reach, not welcoming his touch. "You're still pretending you didn't read it?"

Her rejection speared him through. "*Sam—*"

"Fine. I'll play along. Let's pretend that you didn't read it." She gestured to the envelope, crossing her arms so tight she should have cracked. "Do it now. See if you got your money's worth."

He shook his head, his heart twisting.

"Open it, or I walk out *right now*," she said, hands fisted.

He took a step toward her, anger rushing through his veins at her ultimatum. He tried to calm it, tried to shut it down, but it ignored his commands. "That's not fair."

"Life's not fair," she countered. "See what he found. Maybe you're right and my secret is safe."

Jaw tight, he snatched it up angrily, ripping the papers out of the crisp envelope. He skimmed the words, hoping to find no details of her life, for her sake, but the cover page alone summed up everything she had already told him, and then some. His heart sank.

"Well?"

For the first time in as long as he could remember, he was at a loss for words.

She laughed, clearly not needing any. "See? Told you."

"Still, no one would know who you are or care enough to dig into your past."

She rolled her eyes. "Every single woman in your circle feels like they have a claim on you, and I assure you they would investigate my past even faster than your detective the second you claimed me as yours in public. Why do you think I told you that we wouldn't work?"

"Fuck that and fuck them."

"So you'd be okay with publicly attaching yourself to a family of embezzlers," she asked, searching his face for something he wasn't sure she really wanted to find. "You'd go to a ball with me, even knowing everyone would find out the truth, and hold your head high, even though your investors might bail because of me? Even though, if the truth came out, I could affect your company, your life, your *choices*?"

"I…" He trailed off, his throat aching with the words he wanted to say but couldn't.

She stared at him, tears welling in her eyes.

It wasn't that he was ashamed of her, or that he wouldn't be just as proud of her as he was before the truth came out. It was that he was a business owner, with hundreds of people depending on him for his livelihood, and she asked him a serious question that required thought, something he couldn't rush through, damn it.

This decision would impact more than just himself, so he owed it to his employees to give them more than a split second before promising himself away to the daughter of two criminals.

"This is why I refused to get attached or to open myself up, but you just kept pushing for me to let you close, even though it was a horrible idea," she said, swiping her hands under her eyes. "You just kept being you and making me fall for you."

"*Sam*," he said, too little, too late.

She shook her head, stepping farther away from him.

The added distance resonated inside him, in places he'd never explored.

"It's over," she mumbled.

He caught her hand, refusing to let go this time. "Sam, I—"

"Don't bother trying to explain or make any of this better. None of this is ever going to be better."

"But maybe—" he started, not willing to let her go.

Not until he had a chance to think, damn it.

She grabbed her coat off the couch. "Just let it *go*, Taylor. You did something I could never forgive, and this is done."

He stumbled toward her, tripping over his feet. "Wait—"

She shook her head. "It's done. We're done."

Pain stabbed through his body.

"I don't want you to go," he said, chasing after her. "We can figure this out—"

He reached for her arm, but she yanked free. He scrambled after her, his gut twisting and his chest aching. Losing her was *not* an option.

He'd never known happiness, not until he held her in his arms, naked in his bed, and laughed at something so hard they both cried. Not until they danced in a living room with no music, just because.

Not until he had her.

His fingers slipped through her arm, grasping nothing but air. "*Sam—*"

"Stop!" she cried, stumbling back again, almost falling in her desperation to escape him. "It's over, the date is over. I don't want to be with you anymore. Just let me go!"

He stood still, choking on emotion and unspoken pleas for her to stay as she bolted to the elevator and pushed the button frantically. When this started, he promised not to press her for more than she was willing to give.

One promise he'd made to her had already been broken. He wasn't about to break another.

The doors opened, and she fled into the safety of the metal box as if the devil himself chased after her. As soon as the doors shut and he was alone, he let out an angry yell, picked up the closest thing to him, and chucked it against the wall. It wasn't until the vase shattered, until water and broken petals trailed down the drywall as his chest heaved with each staggered breath, that he realized the uncomfortable truth.

The devil she ran from was *him*.

Chapter Twenty

Three days. That's how long it had been since she left Taylor's apartment and sworn to herself never to go back. Six calls. That's how many times her phone had rung, and she had refused to pick up because, if she did, she might forget what she shouldn't. Four knocks. That's how many times he'd come to her place, begging through her locked door to be let inside, to be given a chance to prove that she hadn't made a mistake in trusting him, that he wanted to be with her, no matter her past. Every time she ignored him was harder than the last.

Each unanswered call hurt more, too.

What made it even worse was that she'd *love* to open that door or pick up that phone, because she wasn't really all that mad at him in the first place for what he did. She'd walked away to protect him...

Not to hurt him.

He'd been scared...but determined to take a risk on her. Putting everything he worked so hard for on the line for a girl he'd been having sex with was *inconceivable*, and she couldn't let him do it. Things would have ended eventually anyway, and she loved him too much to let him ruin his life for her…especially since he didn't, and wouldn't, love her.

She'd hoped that over the course of the weekend she might get over him, but it hadn't happened. She loved him and couldn't be with him. You didn't just *get over* that.

It took *time.*

She glanced at her phone, frowning at the lit-up screen. It wasn't him. She picked up her phone, swiped right, and held it to her ear. "Yes, Mother, I'm fine."

Izzy sighed. "You can't blame me for checking."

"I know." She smiled, playing with a pen on her desk. The pen reminded her of Taylor's persistent theft from his secretary, which stole the smile right off her face. She dropped it, rotating her desk chair so she faced the other way. "And I love you for it."

"Of course, you do." Izzy sniffed. "Are we on for dinner and dancing tonight?"

"Dinner, yes. Dancing, no." She rubbed her forehead. "Nice try, though."

"Come on, I've been trying to get you to go out with me for years. We're both single and hot, so we should be out there having fun. This could be the night where we get drunk, get stupid, flirt with some guys, and dance our asses off until the last song plays."

She frowned. "I don't want to flirt."

"Then don't." Izzy groaned. "But at least dance and drink with me."

She hesitated, thinking of her bleak night at home, alone and likely curled up in bed, crying over Taylor. It wasn't until she lost him that she admitted to herself that she loved him, but that didn't make the pain any less real. That pain, that crippling loss, was taking over her life.

Taylor, meanwhile, was busily hitting up the social scene. Not only had the papers shown him at the gala with Julie, but they'd gone to another event for the fight against childhood cancer. He was burying himself in parties and having a social life, while she was hiding at home in a bathrobe with a box of chocolates.

No more.

"Fine," she gritted.

Izzy gasped. "Seriously? Like, seriously?"

"Don't make me change my mind," Sam warned.

Laughing, Izzy let out a little squeal. "I won't give you a chance to, because we won't be talking again until I pick you up. See you at seven, wear a sexy dress, love you, bye."

Smiling, she said into the dead line, "Love you, too."

There. Take that, Page Six.

She spun her chair back around, frowning at the webpage on her computer that showed Taylor walking out of the museum event with his jacket undone and his hair mussed. Had someone touched his hair, run their fingers through it? Had he moved on to a meaningless one-night stand already? Had she been the only idiot to go and fall in love after promising not to?

It certainly seemed that way.

"Ms. Matthews?" a deep voice said from behind her.

She tore her eyes from her computer and stood in surprise. "Mr. Harper, hi. I'm sorry, I must've forgotten that we had an appointment—"

"We don't," he said, grinning and sitting down. "I just stopped by to thank you."

She sat back down, her gut twisting because if he was thanking her, he'd probably accepted the offer Taylor had given him. She'd lost. Again.

"I spoke to the buyer for my company, as I'd decided to take him up on his generous offer, and before I could accept my terms as-is, he asked if I had your plans on me."

Sam stiffened. "What? Why?"

"He said he wanted to use them when he backed my company and brought it into the next century. He's generously agreed to front the money to get me where I need to be so I have a fighting chance at saving Harper Enterprises. He told me he'd be there to help me every step of the way, and that if I stuck to your plan, I might succeed. If I don't, he'll write off the loan as a failed experiment."

Her heart pounded hard, echoing in her ears. What was Taylor up to now...? "But why would he do that? What's the catch?"

"There isn't any. He told me he wanted to expand his services and that I was the first company he was going to try this new partnership technique on."

Confusion muddled her brain. "Partnership...?"

"Brilliant, right? He also asked me to pass along his card." He reached into his pocket and handed it to her. She accepted it gingerly with shaking fingers, remembering the first time Taylor had tried to give her his business card. "He said to come see him if you have any questions or concerns about the process, and he let me know that he'd be in touch with you personally."

Sam stared down at the card, mentally tracing his name.

"I'm very excited about this future endeavor," he said, rising to his feet again.

She stood, forcing a smile. While she was confused as to what Taylor hoped to gain from this whole thing, this was actually a huge deal for Mr. Harper, and she couldn't help but be happy for him. "As you should be, this is huge."

"I have you to thank for this," he said, shaking her hand. "Well, you and Mr. Jennings. He said it was your impassioned speech you gave him the other night about saving my company that ultimately changed his mind about liquidating it and reassigning my employees."

"It was nothing." *Actually, I had no idea about it at all.*

"I'm happy Harper Enterprises will live to see another day, sir."

"Me too." He pushed the chair back into place. "I better go tell Martha. She'll be so happy."

The smile on her face was real, despite the ache inside her—ugh, she'd have to *talk* to him, now that he bought Harper Enterprises. "I bet. We'll talk later."

He waved and walked away while she sat at her desk, staring at the tiny piece of rectangular card stock. She tapped her fingers on her thighs, debating the best course of action. An email? A text? A short, professional phone call? Email. Definitely email. She pulled her keyboard out, fully intending to take the coward's way out of speaking to him.

Dear Mr. Jennings,
It has come to my attention that you used my plan to save Mr. Harper's company without my consent—

She backspaced that whole sentence.

Dear Mr. Jennings,
Thank you for your attention to the Harper Enterprises case, and your unwanted help—

Again. Delete.

Dear Taylor,
I love you. I miss you. Fuck you.

She aggressively deleted that one.

"Sam!" her boss, Jessica, called, waving at her excitedly.

Sam jumped out of her skin, quickly closed the email, and stood with a racing heart. She'd never seen her stalwart boss so...so...happy. "Yes—?"

"I just got off the phone with Mr. Jennings from Jennings Consolidations. When he called me at home this weekend, I almost hung up on him, but when he informed me that he was buying Harper Enterprises and asked for permission to contact you with any questions pertaining to your business plan, I could have kissed the man. What a great move, for us *and* Mr. Harper."

"I—" Sam started.

"Mr. Harper was certainly pleased with the end results. With Mr. Jennings's financial backing and expertise, hopefully this works, and we will be able to convince him to help more companies stay solvent or accept a buyout, whichever is best for them."

Her heart picked up speed, because she was right. It was a huge move for *everyone.*

"I even got him to agree to consider more cases such as Mr. Harper's in the future," Jessica said in a rush. "I'd like you to be his personal contact in all of this. If we catch his interest with another company, you can draft the reports, since he liked your style so much."

Sam swallowed hard. "Uh…"

"He said he attended a few galas and got some backers over the weekend, but he wants to go to the Mertz Fundraiser tomorrow evening to make an official announcement. I told him I wouldn't miss it for the world, but I thought it would be a good idea for you to go, too, to help represent us in this new endeavor. Mr. Jennings wasn't sure you'd be able to make it, but I told him I couldn't *imagine* you missing it. The color scheme is red. You have something red to wear, right?"

She forced a smile, not really seeing any way around this. Either she could admit she didn't want to go because she'd slept with their new friend, and ruin her chances at helping people, or she would have to come up with another believable reason not to—AKA *lie.*

And she didn't like lying.

"He did say not to feel pressured to come along. He was very adamant that you not come if you didn't want to," Jessica added, studying Sam a little too closely. "Do you?"

"I wouldn't miss it for the world," Sam said through clenched teeth masked behind a smile. Despite her feelings for Taylor, this was a huge step for their company and so many others out there who needed a little help. "Honestly, I'd love to come."

"Excellent." She smiled even wider. "Do us proud, Sam."

"I will," she promised, her heart picking up even more speed at the prospect of going out with Taylor in public. Why had he done this? Was this some sort of message to her? Did this mean…? No. It meant nothing. Nothing had changed. She was still her, and he was still him.

The second she was alone, she pulled the email up again.

If they were going to go out, she wanted a moment or two alone with him first before getting thrust into the midst of her coworkers and his.

She stared at the greeting, forcing herself to leave it as-is, and added:

Dear Mr. Jennings,

It would appear that we're kind of in business together and are attending the same event tomorrow. I feel no pressure to attend but will be doing so as it's best for my company. See you there.

Professionally,
Ms. Matthews

She hovered over the send button but eventually hit it. Within thirty seconds, she had a reply. Heartbeat echoing in her head, she clicked on the email.

Sam,

I've always loved you in red. I'm still looking forward to our second date.

With love,
Taylor

She didn't know what hit her the hardest: that he'd ignored all her professional cues and formalities, that he'd mentioned a second date, or that he'd thrown in the "L" word. *Twice.*

Shaking her head, she left his email unanswered and grabbed her coat and purse. She had a red dress to buy, and it was going to be one hell of a dress, not because of who she was going out with, but because it was for a fancy work event, and she had to play the part.

And if she told herself that enough times…

She just might believe it.

Chapter Twenty-One

"I think it's good, Mom."

"Almost...there..." His mother fussed over his red bow tie, tightening it until he shrunk into a tiny kid on Christmas Eve getting dressed for church all over again. He winced, swallowing experimentally. He could still do that, so breathing remained an option. She smiled, her wrinkled face lighting up when she stepped back to admire her handiwork. "Perfect."

Yeah, sure it was, if perfect meant suffocating...

"Thanks."

Seven thirty-one. Jesus, his stomach was a tangled ball of nerves.

He'd done a hell of a lot of thinking and soul-searching after he lost Sam, and he'd come up with the perfect gesture to show her just how much she meant to him. Hopefully it was enough.

"Don't be nervous," his mom said, touching his cheek tenderly. His mother was so short, barely five feet tall, but somehow, she would always seem larger than life to him. She had done so much for him—given so much for him—and he'd never repay that. "This Sam girl won't be able to resist you when she sees you all dressed up like this."

He'd told his mom about Sam and the way he'd lost her, and she had been nothing but supportive and excited over the fact that her son had finally met a woman he wanted to be with. "I hope you're right, but she's not exactly the 'swooning' type. Getting her to forgive me will be a lot harder than being nicely dressed when she shows up."

"Then it's a good thing you have more of a plan than skating by with your handsome face," she teased. "I can't wait to meet her. Don't forget dinner at my place next Friday."

He shook his head. "If I get her to give me another—"

"*When*." She pointed at him. "What did I teach you about the power of positive thinking?"

He barely refrained from groaning. He loved his mother, but sometimes she was too much. "When I get her back, I'll talk to her about it."

"I'll order Mexican, since it'll be Friday."

He checked his reflection, holding his breath. "Order whatever you want, Mom."

"Really?"

He nodded absentmindedly.

Was his hair sticking up in the back?

Shit, he'd never been this goddamn nervous before. Everything about Sam set him on edge, threatened his control, and challenged his way of living—and he couldn't live without her messing up his plans for another minute. "Wish me luck."

"You won't need it."

He kissed his mother's head. "I ordered a car to take you home."

She nodded, picking up the envelope and pocket-sized planner on the table. "Don't forget these."

He'd almost forgotten the most important part of the evening. Shaking his head at himself, he said one more farewell to his mother, got in the elevator, and found his ride. He really didn't want the first time seeing her again to be in a public setting, with all eyes on him. Maybe he should drop by her place, all casual-like, and offer her a ride there. He could play it off cool and test the waters. See if she hated him as much as he hated himself.

"To the gala, Mr. Jennings?" his driver asked, watching him through the rearview mirror.

Taylor checked the time, hesitating. "Actually…"

By the time the car pulled up to her building, he was even more of a mess than he'd been in his apartment, because he wasn't sure if this was the right move. With Sam, he never had a fucking clue what he was doing, so it wasn't a surprise that this was the case *again*. He was a fighter, a winner, and he didn't give up on anything until he got the outcome he sought.

Normally, when he saw something, he wanted it, he got it. End of story.

Gritting his teeth, he tucked the small envelope into his jacket, opened the car door, and stepped out onto the curb. As he approached the building, the door opened, and a blonde that he recognized instantly as Sam's friend from the coffee shop stepped out, carrying a makeup bag and a pink blow-dryer. She stopped, giving him a frown.

He bowed at her, smiling despite her obvious disapproval. "Izzy, right?"

"Yeah." She hugged her bag. "Taylor, right?"

"Yep." He nodded, stepping around her. "It was nice seeing—"

She moved in his path. "What are you doing here?"

"I wanted to offer her a ride—" He broke off because that was a bullshit response. "I want to win her back."

"Don't hurt her," she said, looking him up and down.

"I won't," he vowed. "I swear, if she'll let me, I'll spend the rest of my life making her happy. There's nothing I want more."

She softened a little bit, her mouth not quite so thinly held. "She's pretty set in her decision to be single."

"I know." His stomach tightened even more. "But I'm not."

Shrugging, she moved out of his way. "Good luck."

"Yeah." His heart pounded even harder. "Thanks."

Taylor walked to her door. Before he could knock, it swung open, and Sam stood there in a long red dress that hugged every curve of her body as if it had been created solely for her by some expensive designer in Paris—something that wasn't possible, because his Sam would never be that frivolous. Her long hair was swept back and gathered at the base of her neck, and soft curls fell over her shoulder and down her chest. She wore red lipstick, dark eyeshadow, and should've been on the cover of a magazine rather than on his arm.

As she caught sight of him, she stumbled back, eyes wide.

"Wow. You're absolutely stunning," he managed to say.

Funny, though, his voice sounded foreign.

"Thanks." She blushed. "What are you doing here, Taylor?"

She was a princess. A goddess. The woman he wanted to spend the rest of his life with...and he couldn't seem to string two words together coherently. "I mean it. You're far too beautiful to be seen with me at your side. You deserve better than me."

She stepped back, letting him in. "Let's not be dramatic."

"I love how you always call me on my bullshit," he said as he closed the door behind him.

She stiffened and turned away.

"I brought you something."

She faced him. "I don't want anything from you."

"Here." He handed her the calendar. "Open it."

She stared at it, then flipped it open to the current month. She lifted her head, her forehead creased with confusion. "What—?"

"See those circled dates?"

She lowered her head again. "Yeah…"

"Those dates are days I think we should go out together. Dinner, a movie, a show, whatever you'd like. It's up to you."

She stared at the book, trembling, and slammed it shut. She set it down on the coffee table, not looking at it again, even going so far as to put some distance between her and the planner. "Taylor…"

"Don't say no. Not yet. Think about it," he said, smoothing his tux and stopping her from whatever rejection she had been about to slam down. "How have you been?"

"Fine," she said, her voice hollow.

He gritted his teeth. "I hate that word."

"Sorry." She crossed her arms and faced him again. She always did that when she was nervous, as if the gesture could somehow protect her from anything he might say. "I went dancing with Izzy last night at some loud, smelly club. Some dude invited me back to his place."

Jealousy hit him hard. He had no right to be jealous, though. He'd lost that right when she broke up with him. And yet…he couldn't stop himself from asking, "Did you go home with him?"

"No." She lifted her chin, squaring her jaw. "I could have, though. I could have gone home with him, had sex, and tried to forget about you."

Relief punched him in the gut, warring with the pain that had been his constant companion since losing her. "I know."

"Why are you doing this?" She tightened her grip on

her arms. "Why invest in that company and plan this whole thing?"

"Because you changed me," he said quietly. "I want to do better. Be better. I want to save some companies, not just rip them apart. I want to be a man who is worthy of you."

She sucked in a breath, lowering her lids. "Don't."

"Don't what?" he asked, taking another step.

He was close now—close enough to smell her floral perfume and shampoo. Something clamped around his heart, squeezing, and it was hard to breathe.

"Talk like that," she said, her voice cracking. "Nothing has changed. We can't just pick up where we left off."

"Why not?" he said, not moving any closer.

"Because I'm me, and you don't deserve to be dragged—" she said, closing her eyes.

"You're right, I don't deserve you, but not the way you mean. I don't deserve you because you're far too good for me." This time he took a tiny step. "Far too good for anyone."

She shook her head. "I—"

"I'm going to be honest here, Sam. I want to be with you, and I don't give a damn what anyone else might think or say about it," he admitted. "Nothing has changed for me. You're still the one woman I want to break all my rules for."

She shook her head. "You don't. Not really."

"How would you know?"

She bit her lip hard. "Because once the truth came out and everyone knew who I really was, you would be dragged down into the dirt with me, and once you were there, you'd realize the mistake you made, and you'd regret it…but it would be too late to take it back."

"That's not true," he vowed, moving slightly closer. His heart pounded against his ribs. She backed up a step, maintaining the distance between them. "I would never regret a single second at your side."

She pressed her lips together. "You say that now, but—"

"I regret a lot of things, though. Like how I got that stupid fucking report—"

She waved a hand. "You had to find out somehow, and it might as well have been like that. I was going to tell you anyway."

"You…forgive me?"

She nodded, not meeting his eyes. "I do. To be honest, I'm not even mad about it."

He blinked. "Wait. What?"

"That's not why I walked away that night."

He cleared his throat. He'd been all prepared to beg for her forgiveness on his knees if need be, and he didn't even *have* to? "You're not mad at me?"

"You're a good man. I've known that for a long time, and for me to hold a grudge against you is like being mad at the clouds for raining. It's just not possible. I was very mysterious about the whole thing and refused to talk. I understand the temptation to investigate it and can see why you did it."

A big weight lifted off his shoulders, and he grinned, taking a step toward her. "Then can we give it another try? I swear this time, I'll—"

"No." She held a hand up, her eyes watery. "Like I said, you're a good man, and you deserve the best. You have it all planned out, your whole life, and I'm just a complication—"

"The hell you are," he growled. He'd had this whole speech prepared, but all that went right out the window the second she said that. Picking up his planner, he walked over to the kitchen and tossed it in the garbage. "Fuck plans, and fuck calendars. I'll take 'complications' over that shit any day, any time, as long as they come with you."

Her jaw dropped. "Taylor—"

Closing the distance between them, he didn't take his time or allow her to stop him. He didn't control each step or take a second to think.

Not this time. Not with her.

Without a word, without a warning, he wrapped his arms around her and caught her chin. "I knew, nearly from the beginning, that you were special, that you were in a category all your own. You challenge me, you force me to be spontaneous, and you help me see how I can make the world a better place. I didn't propose this deal with Mr. Harper as a way to force you to work with me or stay in my life. I did it because I *believe* in you. You make me believe in unicorns."

She choked on a laugh. "And rainbows?"

"Motherfucking rainbows." He caressed her back. "I shouldn't have hesitated that night when you asked me if I still wanted to be with you."

She bit her lower lip. "Yes, you should've."

"You're wrong." He pressed his thumb to the spot she'd bitten. "Next time you ask me if I'm by your side, I won't hesitate to say yes. My answer will always be yes."

She fisted his shirt. "Taylor—"

"Shh." He pressed a finger to her mouth. "Let me finish. Yes, I want you. Yes, I choose you. Yes, I would do anything you asked me to do. Yes, I miss you. Yes, I want you back. Yes, I would walk through fire for you. Yes, I'd rescue a unicorn for you. Yes, I l—"

She laughed, resting a hand on his chest. "There you go, being dramatic again."

"Only for you, Sam." He lowered his face, stopping short of kissing her. "Only with you."

She let out a puff of air. "But—"

"No buts. No fucking *buts*." He gritted his teeth. "I want to be with you. I want you at my side, everywhere, and nothing will change my mind. Not your past. Nothing that could ever happen in the future. No matter what, I want you. The question is…do you want me?"

Chapter Twenty-Two

She closed her eyes, taking a page out of his book, and counted to ten. God, she wanted to say yes, to take what he was offering and run with it. He was fully aware of what he was taking on, and if he was willing to do that, to be with her despite her tarnished past, why not say yes?

Was it wrong to be with the man she loved?

People did inexplicable things when in love. They overlooked flaws, habits, addictions, differences, money, class, distinction—when those things went up against love, they usually lost.

She loved him. She wanted to be with him.

End of story.

She stared into the deep green depths of his eyes. Had they always been this light? So bright? "The fifteenth."

He frowned. "What about it?"

"You and I will be attending the SPCA fundraiser. It's a black-tie event."

A smile lit up his face. "I'd say that I'll put it in the calendar, but…"

She smiled, because more than likely he'd be fishing that bad boy out of the garbage. It was a nice gesture and all, but he needed it. "We'll go camping after."

That smile went away immediately. "O…kay…"

"Just kidding."

"Thank God," he groaned.

"But in all seriousness, if we do this…it's going to be more than before, Taylor. More than soft whispers, empty promises, and a fun first date. I want those dates you circled in the calendar to be real dates. A third, and a fourth, and a fifth. If we do this, if we try again, it's for *real* this time. No games to lighten it, no pretending it's all one big date. Just you and me, making this real. Real commitment. Real feelings."

He touched her cheek. "Sam—"

"And no more going to events with other women. You don't share, and neither do I."

His mouth twitched, and he skimmed his fingers over her lower lip. "Any other terms?"

"I want you to wear a unicorn shirt out in public once."

He laughed—a full-blown, hearty laugh that warmed her soul. "Only if you wear a shark one at the same time."

"Deal."

"You know…" He skimmed his finger over her mouth again, and she shivered. "Every time I'm with you, it's like I'm on the edge of a cliff, and your hands are on my back. I'm not sure whether you're going to push me off or pull me to safety, but either way I know I'll be all right, because I've got you, and you've got me, and that's all that matters, right?"

"I'd never push you," she breathed. "I'll always pull you closer."

"I broke a promise to you," he admitted.

She swallowed. "Enough about that stupid report. I—"

"Not that one," he whispered, kissing the spot he'd just wiped dry. "I promised not to fall for you."

She held her breath. "I promised the same thing."

"I promised a lot of things back when we first got together, but I'm going to make different ones now. I promise to be there for you, in public and private, in any way you want. I promise to treat you as the most important person in my life and to always work hard to deserve you, because you're so much better of a person than I am. And I promise to love you for the rest of my life, Sam." Locking eyes with her, he cradled her face with his large palms and smiled at her. That smile stole her breath away before his words could. "I love you."

A small sound that she didn't recognize escaped her, and she lurched up on her tiptoes to kiss him. Fisting his tuxedo jacket, she clung to the only thing holding her down on the ground right now: *him*. Even on her toes, she was at least four inches shorter than his towering frame. Tears wet her cheeks as she ended the kiss, sucking in a deep breath. "I love you, too," she breathed.

He froze.

"When I lost you…it hurt so much I thought I was going to die," she admitted in a broken whisper. "I never want to go through that again."

"Now who's the dramatic one?" A smile teased at his lips as he continued backing her toward the wall.

Her heart skipped a beat because the second they reached it, he'd lift her up, step between her thighs, and bring her to heights she'd missed more than anything over these last few days. "Me," she said, smiling.

The kiss deepened as her back hit the wall, and his hands under her butt supported her weight as he stepped between her thighs. His fingers slid where she needed him most. The second he pressed against her, they both groaned. Her because she wanted him, and him as he ended the kiss and took his fingers away. "Shit."

"What?" she asked impatiently, trying to kiss him again.

He avoided her mouth, arching his neck as she nipped the skin under his ear, since it was all she could reach. "We have to go." He tightened his hold on her hips. "The driver is outside."

She sighed, dropping her head back and gripping his shoulders. "Can we send him away?"

"Unfortunately, no." He stepped back, his fingers lingering over her butt as he lowered her to her feet. "It's time to make our first official appearance together as a couple."

She tugged on her gown, smoothing it, her heart dropping like an anvil. "Are you su—?"

"If you ask me if I'm sure again, I might lose my temper." He cradled her face, his soft touch at direct contrast with his words. "What did I tell you my answer would be?"

"Yes, always yes," she whispered.

He nodded, dropping his forehead to hers.

Her heart was so full with love and happiness it was a miracle it didn't burst or lift her off the floor like a balloon. "I love you," she said.

"I'll never get sick of hearing that," he rasped, kissing her again, but unfortunately keeping it short and sweet. "I love you, too. Now come on. I'm ready to show the world you're mine."

Smiling, she let him drag her out the door, only stopping long enough to grab her jacket and her purse. After they were settled in the back seat of the SUV he'd ordered, he touched his tux jacket pocket nervously, clearing his throat.

"So I pulled something together for you, in case you were interested. Please don't think you have to accept this, but you were so upset when my investigator found out your past, and you said all you wanted was a clean slate."

She frowned. "Okay..."

"Well, I got you one, if you want it," he said, handing

her an envelope. "If you want him to, my guy can make it so that whoever searches you up, no matter how good they are, they'll only find what is in that envelope, if that's what you want."

She opened it, her heart beating fast.

As she unfolded the paper, her eyes widened, because according to the background check in front of her, she'd grown up in Georgia, lived a normal, boring life, attended private school, and moved to Chicago for college and stayed. No stories of her parents, no mention of a name change, nothing, just boring stuff no one would read twice.

"How...?"

He covered her knee with his hand. "Connections and money. I mean, it probably wouldn't hold up against the cops or anything, but as long as you don't get arrested, you could have your clean slate. Not because I want it, I don't care if you go around telling everyone in that party tonight what your parents did, I'll be right there with you, but if you want it... it's yours."

She blinked rapidly, holding the paper to her chest.

"I know it was presumptuous of me to start this without asking, but he hasn't done anything official yet. He just mocked up a report of what your past would look like." He laughed, running a hand through his hair. "He said it was best if we didn't know too much, but you can apparently do wonders by just breaching a few firewalls."

"You'd do that?" she asked slowly, blinking, still hugging the paper. "For me?"

"I'd do anything for you, Sammy."

The love she'd been hiding choked her, welling up in her chest so much it was a miracle she didn't explode. It threatened to spill out if she dared open her mouth to speak, so she kissed him.

He curled his hand around the nape of her neck, holding

her in place as his mouth worked over hers. The car stopped, and he ended the kiss, sighing. "Interrupted, again."

"Thank you," she whispered. Reluctantly, she handed it back, smiling. "It means the world to me that you would do that, but I can't let you break the law for me."

"Are you sure—?"

She touched his mouth, nodding. "I wanted a clean slate, yes, and I got it, with you. If someone digs up my past, screw them. The only person I care about is right here, in this car with me, and he loves me no matter what."

He nodded, kissing her again. "Yes, he does."

"So…" She tipped her head toward the building filled with rich people. "Fuck them."

Laughing, he nodded at the driver as he opened their car door.

She got out, and the second his feet hit the sidewalk, his hand closed over hers. With his other hand, he tucked the fake report in his pocket. She took a deep breath, tipping her head back to stare at the top of the skyscraper. "Are you ready for this?"

He tightened his fingers on hers reassuringly. "What did I say?"

"Yes," she breathed, her heart filling even more. "Always yes."

Epilogue

One year later

They sat on his couch (*their* couch, now), cuddled in the corner, his arms around her as they sipped wine in front of the crackling fireplace. They'd given up the pretense of her having her own place six months ago and had been happily living together ever since. Since she didn't like opulence and her place wasn't big enough for the two of them, they'd compromised and bought an affordable yet comfortable cottage on the outskirts of the city. It had three bedrooms, two bathrooms, and was very sensible.

Gone were the days of penthouses and million-dollar trips.

It was Saturday, so they'd started out at Habitat for Humanity, then the soup kitchen, and ended up at their favorite restaurant—Fado Irish Pub—and finally, they'd gone to see a show. Taylor pulled out their calendar of dates, setting it on her lap.

"Want to mark today off for me?" he asked, handing her

a marker.

She frowned at it. "Since when did you start carrying one of these again?"

He'd truly given up his schedules when they'd become official. They ate whatever they wanted, whenever they wanted, and he no longer lived as a slave to his calendar.

"Just open it," he murmured, pressing his mouth to her temple and kissing it.

She huddled closer to his chest and opened the pages, which had been paper clipped to open on November. She found the twenty-second and crossed it off with an X and frowned. "Why does it say see next calendar?"

"Does it?" he asked as if he had no idea—yet it was in his writing.

"What are you up to?" she murmured, craning her neck to see him and touching his unshaven jaw.

He'd participated in No-Shave November this year at her request, and she was fully enjoying the fuzz...though she wouldn't mind when he shaved it all off and she could see his hard jawline again. "Nothing," he said, pulling another calendar out of his back pocket.

She took it, frowning at it. "Have you been carrying that around all day?"

"Call me Hamilton."

She blinked. "Why?"

He shrugged a shoulder, taking a big sip of wine. "The dude knows what he wants and doesn't stop until he gets it."

She rolled her eyes. "And you want a calendar? If you wanted to bring them back into our lives, you could have just said it."

He laughed. "It's not that."

"Then what?"

He tipped his head toward the item in her hand. "Open it."

Glancing down, her heart skipped a beat. She was almost afraid to see what was inside. The past year had been the best year of her life. He'd swept her off her feet that night at her old apartment, and he hadn't let her touch the ground again. They had a few fights, sure, but each time they made up, it drew them closer to each other, and she couldn't imagine her life without him in it. What if whatever was in here threw that balance off?

What if she was greedy to hope for more?

He cleared his throat and reached into his back pocket again, not removing his hand. It wouldn't have been weird in any other circumstance, but sitting like they were on the couch, with her on his lap...it looked less than comfortable, to say the least. "Open it."

"Okay..." She opened it. There were no markings, no mentions of meetings. It was completely bare except— she stopped flipping through at the date circled in pink. "What...?"

He slid out from under her and fell to one knee. It took her a full three seconds to figure out why, and when she did, she dropped the book and covered her mouth.

Smiling nervously, he held the diamond ring up. "This is the last time I'll ever circle a date in my planner, but it felt way too huge to not do so."

She swallowed, pressing her hand more fully to her mouth.

"So...I was thinking, if you're not too busy that day, you might like to spend the day wearing a dress. I'll wear a tux. But there's one condition."

She nodded for him to continue, not speaking because there were no words inside of her right now. Just incoherent squealing and shrieking.

"You have to promise, in front of everyone, to be mine for the rest of our lives. I love you so much, more than I ever thought possible, and the only way I could be any happier is if you did me the honor of being my wife." He swallowed, his hand shaking slightly, which only made her eyes tear up even more, because Taylor *never* trembled. "Sam, will you marry me?"

She lowered her hands, tears streaming down her cheeks. "What did you say your answer would always be to me?"

"I..." He swallowed again. "I want to hear you say it."

"Yes." She sat up and swung her knees over the side of the couch, covering his hand with both of hers. "Always yes."

He closed the distance between them, kissing her, and she clung to him with her eyes shut and her heart pounding so loudly she couldn't hear the internal shrieking anymore.

When he pulled back, he gently slid the ring on her finger, running his hand over her knuckle. "I love you, Sam. So damn much."

"I love you, too."

He kissed her again, and as he lowered her on the couch and slid his body over hers, she thanked God that a year ago, she'd been too distracted and bid on the wrong man, because he was, hands down, the best mistake she'd *ever* made.

About the Author

Diane Alberts is a multi-published, bestselling contemporary romance author with Entangled Publishing. She also writes *New York Times* and *USA Today* bestselling new adult books under the name Jen McLaughlin. She's hit the Top 100 lists on Amazon and Barnes and Noble numerous times with numerous titles. Diane is represented by Louise Fury at The Bent Agency. Her goal is to write so many fantastic stories that even a non-romance reader will know her name. Diane has always been a dreamer with a vivid imagination, but it wasn't until 2011 that she put her pen where her brain was, and became a published author. Since receiving her first contract offer, she has yet to stop writing. Though she lives in the mountains, she really wishes she was surrounded by a hot, sunny beach with crystal clear water. She lives in Northeast Pennsylvania with her four kids, a husband, a schnauzer mutt, and four cats.

Discover more category romance titles from Entangled Indulgence...

CATCHING THE CEO
a *Billionaire's Second Chance* novel by Victoria Davies

Billionaire Damien Reid can barely believe it when Caitlyn Brooks shows up at the conference reception. He has no desire to spend a moment longer with the infuriating woman than he has to. Except he can't seem to stop his eyes from following her or the unnerving need to ruffle her perfect feathers. When teasing turns to touching, he's not sure if it's the best or worst mistake of his life.

SCOTLAND OR BUST
a *Winning the Billionaire* novel by Kira Archer

After dumping her boyfriend, Nicole Franklin jumps on a plane and heads to Europe. Sure, money and a job would have been nice to line up first. Even a visa, for that matter. So now she has to play tour guide at an Outlander experience for the most obnoxious man on the planet. Until she stumbles into the wrong bed in the middle of the night and wakes up in Harrison's arms. Now his family thinks they're engaged, and the entire village is betting on how long before she runs for the hills.

THE BILLIONAIRE IN HER BED
a *Worthington Family* novel by Regina Kyle

Real estate mogul Eli Ward knows he has a fight on his hands with his latest project. He doesn't expect that fight to be led by Brooke Worthington, the woman who rocked his world one unforgettable night. The one woman who doesn't know who he is, which is a good thing. Graphic designer and part-time bartender Brooke Worthington refuses to follow her family's plan for her. She's too busy building her artistic career. She doesn't have time for relationships, either, because she has to save the building she lives in from some greedy real estate billionaire.

CPSIA information can be obtained
at www.ICGtesting.com
Printed in the USA
LVHW042124161222
735374LV00002B/259